PLAYING DIRTY

A J.J. GRAVES MYSTERY

LILIANA HART

To Scott—You were an amazing help on this book. Thank you from the bottom of my heart. Your cycling knowledge is beyond compare, and I have a great appreciation for you in Spandex. I love you and appreciate you, even though you say my name over and over while my headphones are on and I'm on deadline.

ACKNOWLEDGMENTS

A huge thanks to my editors, Imogen Howson and Ava Hodge, and my cover designer Dar Albert.

Thank you to my children for being self-sufficient and knowing how to order pizza and Uber Eats when I forget dinner.

And always, thank you, Scott. You're the best partner, husband, sounding board, and police consultant a woman could ask for. I am blessed beyond measure.

Any mistakes are mine alone.

ALSO BY LILIANA HART

JJ Graves Mystery Series

Dirty Little Secrets

A Dirty Shame

Dirty Rotten Scoundrel

Down and Dirty

Dirty Deeds

Dirty Laundry

Dirty Money

A Dirty Job

Dirty Devil

Playing Dirty

Dirty Martini

Addison Holmes Mystery Series

Whiskey Rebellion

Whiskey Sour

Whiskey For Breakfast

Whiskey, You're The Devil

Whiskey on the Rocks

Whiskey Tango Foxtrot

Whiskey and Gunpowder

Whiskey Lullaby

The Scarlet Chronicles

Bouncing Betty

Hand Grenade Helen

Front Line Francis

The Harley and Davidson Mystery Series

The Farmer's Slaughter

A Tisket a Casket

I Saw Mommy Killing Santa Claus

Get Your Murder Running

Deceased and Desist

Malice in Wonderland

Tequila Mockingbird

Gone With the Sin

Grime and Punishment

Blazing Rattles

A Salt and Battery

Curl Up and Dye

First Comes Death Then Comes Marriage

Box Set 1

Box Set 2

Box Set 3

The Gravediggers

The Darkest Corner

Gone to Dust

Say No More

I am no bird; and no net ensnares me;
I am a free human being with an
    independent will.

—*Charlotte Bronte*

A part of fate is the freedom of man.
Forever wells up the impulse of
 choosing and acting in his soul.

—*Ralph Waldo Emerson*

PROLOGUE

BRETT JORGENSON DIDN'T START HIS DAY BY thinking about death.

He woke before dawn, as he did every morning, leaving his wife snoring softly in their bed. He'd never tell her, but the further along she got in her pregnancy, the more her snoring kept him awake. Earplugs had become his lifesaver.

The house creaked and groaned around him as he padded his way around the room, gathering his clothes he'd laid out the night before, and then headed to the bathroom. He loved the stillness of the morning, the gentle hush of his surroundings as nature, animal, and human all slept.

It was why they'd moved to King George County— the simple life. They wanted their children to enjoy swing sets instead of subways. And moving from the city had been the right decision for all of them. It had saved his family, and he'd do it again if given the choice. The decisions he'd made in his life hadn't always been good or right, but this one was.

Life was as perfect as it could get. There were no phone calls or emails or business meetings. Those would come later. But this time was for himself and the open road to freedom. If there was a God—and he had to think there must be—then Brett imagined he had a little slice of heaven right here on earth.

His blood sang with anticipation. Every morning brought new opportunities—new possibilities—and he went to bed each night eager for the morning. Once he'd brushed his teeth and washed the sleep from his eyes, he put on his cycling bib and leg warmers, and then he strapped on his heart monitor and pulled on his jersey. He left it unzipped as he made his way to the kitchen.

He wasn't one of those people who was controlled by caffeine. He didn't use anything to stimulate his mind or his body. Not anymore. He'd been living clean for eight years, six months, and two days.

He turned off the alarm and headed to the garage where his carbon fiber Trek hung on the wall. He'd filled up his water bottles after his ride with the team the previous night, and they were already in the cages attached to his bike. He loved the routine of cycling.

There was the softest hint of gray in the sky—a pearly incandescent sheen that brought a chill on this November morning. He only had a matter of weeks to ride before the weather would keep him off the roads. But for now—for now it was glorious.

His clip-in shoes sat on the rack against the wall and he slipped them on quickly, securing the Velcro as his flesh pebbled with cold. Even the way he put his shoes on was routine, and he enjoyed the monotony of it as he rolled the bike out of the garage, his shoes clacking against the concrete, and then closed the door behind him. He zipped his jersey, secured his phone in the front pouch, and strapped on his helmet securely before straddling the bike.

The cold wouldn't dissipate as his blood heated and sweat covered his skin—it would only get colder as the wind whipped across his face and body as he increased his speed. He pulled a neoprene mask from his saddlebag and covered his face, and then he clipped his shoes into the pedals.

There was nothing quite like that first stroke, and then the next, as muscles started to loosen and air burned the lungs. He pedaled down the long driveway and then turned onto the country road, careful to watch for signs of headlights. There was risk in riding at this time of day, but it was worth it to see the sun crest and touch the fields with golden light.

His wife and co-workers didn't understand his obsession, but how could they know unless they felt their pulse race beneath their skin or the wind battering against man and machine? It was freedom and speed. It was as close to flying as he could imagine. A smile stretched across his face as he pedaled harder and faster.

The endless stretch of road rose and fell, and a light sheen of sweat covered his body as his breathing fell into a steady rhythm. He drank greedily from his water bottle to replenish fluids, and then pushed harder as he made his way up the hill, praying his timing was just right.

He crested the hill just as the sun exploded into a cacophony of light and color across the land, and just as he did most mornings, he stopped to watch the wonder of the earth waking up. He laughed and drank the rest of his first bottle of water. Pure joy radiated through his every being, and he raised his arms to the sky as if he was conducting the most magnificent symphony in the universe.

And when the moment passed—at least until he could experience it again the following morning—he hunkered down over the bike and let out a *whoop* as he rocketed down the hill. This was his favorite part of the ride, a series of rolling hills for miles. He pushed himself hard to climb the next hill, noting the fog that had started to creep in with the morning. It wasn't unusual, but he needed to be more aware of his surroundings. There were blind spots, and the drivers of cars were rarely as attentive as they should be.

He flew down the next hill, and started his next climb back up, noting his heart rate on his Garmin screen. It was higher than normal, but he'd been struggling on the climbs more than usual. He hadn't thought the ride from the night before had been too strenuous, but he could feel the strain in his muscles as they started to tighten.

He pushed himself harder. Weakness wasn't acceptable. Life was stressful—the audit and a new baby on the way—but he wouldn't have it any other way. What was the point of living if you didn't push everything you did to the limits?

He let his body rest on the way down the next hill, the fog thickening and leaving a layer of moisture on his clothes. He tried to breathe in, to fill his lungs, but his heart was pounding too heavily in his chest. His body ached. The rushing in his ears was so loud he wouldn't have heard a car if it was right on top of him.

Maybe he was getting sick. Several people in the office had gone home with the flu the week before, and a couple of the riders in his group were no-shows the night before because they'd come down with it as well. It was that time of year.

He decided to reach the peak of the next hill and call Marla to come get him. If he had the flu, pushing his body to exhaustion and dehydrating wasn't the smart thing to do. He'd go home, get a couple of days' rest and rehydrate, and then he'd be back to his normal routine feeling better than ever. It was nothing but a little setback. Life couldn't be all highs without any lows. Just like the hills that were currently kicking his ass.

His feet and legs felt like lead, and he knew he wasn't going to have the strength to pedal up the next hill. But he tried anyway. The fog was thickening, and the loss of his hearing made him disoriented.

He kept pedaling.

His Garmin screen was fogged over, or maybe his vision was blurry, but he knew his heart was pounding too fast—too hard—and then he felt the pop in his chest. Pain like nothing he'd ever experienced exploded through his body and then everything went numb and cold.

Brett got a quick glimpse of the truck coming up behind him in his mirror, but he didn't feel the impact as metal met flesh and carbon fiber. He was already dead.

1

THERE WAS THE KIND OF COLD THAT HAD NOTHING to do with the weather—the kind that seeped into the soul and bones and rested there. A cold that began from the inside and penetrated places that might never be warm again.

My name is J.J. Graves, and I was no stranger to the cold. As a doctor, I knew that shivering was the body's attempt to try to stay warm. But I'd stopped shivering hours ago and lethargy had set in. I'd thought the lethargy would mean sleep, but I'd only been able to stare at the clock on the bedside table, the red numbers clicking the minutes, and then eventually, hours.

I tried to focus on my body. It was a good way to pass the time and think about things other than the reality that was suffocating me. I knew what depression felt like—I'd been there before—and it was all about pushing through from one moment and into the next. I'd thought those days were long past, but boy, had I been wrong.

It had been almost forty-eight hours since the life I thought Jack and I were starting to build had crumbled around us. We'd been through so much in our lives—obstacles so horrendous I was surprised either of us was still alive today. I'd made it through neglect from my parents during childhood, and I'd watched Jack fight for his life when he'd been shot on the job. I'd gone through the grief and anger of my parents' driving their car over a cliff and committing suicide, and I'd watched a man I thought I might spend my life with gunned down in cold blood. I'd been strangled nearly to death, and I'd watched as my father came back from the dead, as bold as he pleased, so he could complicate my future as much as he'd complicated my past. Jack and I had both lost friends along the way. But through it all, we'd always had each other. We'd always clung to each other.

But not this time…this time our house of cards had toppled over something that I'd never thought possible. Wasn't it always the small things that somehow became big things? I trusted Jack with my life. I trusted him with my secrets. But he couldn't say the same about me. Maybe he'd never trusted me at all.

That was the question I was asking myself now. Was everything we had a lie? Had I given Jack my all while he still held a part of himself back from me?

I'd known about the shame in Jack's past—about the child he'd conceived with a woman who thought she and the baby would be better off with another man. Jack had been nineteen at the time and had little to offer, so when the woman had begged him to walk away and not cause problems for her, he'd agreed.

Everyone had a past and the baggage that came with it, and everyone had choices in their lives they wished they'd made differently. It was part of being human, and I couldn't and wouldn't hold Jack's mistakes against him when I had made so many of my own.

He'd told me his secret of the child, and all these years, we'd not spoken of it. I'd all but forgotten it had happened, it seemed so long ago. But someone had given the information to Floyd Parker at the *Gazette*, and in a small conservative place like King George, scandals like this were still a big deal. I didn't know if Jack would win the election or not, but I had to believe that the people of King George County had better sense than to let someone like Floyd Parker become their sheriff.

I hadn't betrayed Jack to Floyd or the press. I would never do such a thing, even inadvertently. But that had been the first thought in Jack's mind when the news had been splashed across the front page of the newspaper—that the betrayal had come from me.

It was all in the timing, of course. The election was only a few days away, and Floyd had played his hand brilliantly. We'd just come off a case and whether Jack wanted to admit it or not, the politics of the job were getting to him, so stress was at an all-time high.

Floyd Parker had made it a point to be the bane of our existence and cause chaos and division however he could. He'd succeeded. Now Jack and I were more divided than we'd ever been. The gossip mill was working overtime, especially now that it had gotten out that I was sleeping at the funeral home.

I wasn't really sure how I'd gotten to this place in my life. It was surreal. Me, only married a few months, and already my husband thought the worst of me and I was left with no one on my side. If I had the energy I would've laughed. It seemed to be a recurring theme in my life. Maybe one day there'd be someone who supposedly loved me enough to believe in me unequivocally, but so far, it hadn't been my parents or the love of my life, so I didn't hold out much hope.

Rehashing the memory of my last moments with Jack did nothing but make me sink further into the abyss, so I went back to human anatomy.

I started at my toes, wiggling them slowly, and I was conscious of the nubby sheets scraping against my skin. Then I moved up, visualizing the skeletal system and the tendons, muscles, and vascular system that made me who I was. My pulse was slow and sluggish, and my muscles were tight. I could feel the threat of a charley horse in my calves as I stretched and flexed.

Up the body I went—*vastus medialis, vastus lateralis, iliotibial band, rectus femoris*—I tried to relax each muscle, but I found the task impossible. *Gluteus medius, rectus abdominis, external oblique…*

When I finished, I repeated the exercise over again, and when the clock finally turned to five, with great effort, I pushed back the covers and dragged my legs so they hung over the side of the bed.

The carpet was threadbare on the third floor of the funeral home. Though to be fair, the entire third floor was threadbare. It hadn't been renovated in fifty years, and the last people to live there had been my grandparents. At least until my grandmother had taken a plunge from her bedroom window. Not the one I was currently staying in. I wasn't that macabre. Whether she'd jumped or been pushed, no one knew, but the third floor had been closed off, the furniture draped in white cloths, and mothballs had been put in all the closets.

Over the years, the third floor had become my sanctuary when I had something to hide from. It was the first place I ran when life got hard. Maybe because it was a conscious reminder that, no matter how hard life got, I wouldn't end up like my grandmother. Or maybe it was because I had nowhere else to go.

I got to my feet, the stretch and pull of muscles making me feel much older than my three-plus decades. I was still in my clothes from the day before. Changing had seemed trivial. But I pulled on a thick robe to help with the chill as I opened the door to the bedroom and stepped out into the hall.

I wasn't the only occupant of the funeral home. As far as weeks went, it hadn't been my favorite. There were two bodies, each in a different viewing room and ready for burial, that had been the victims of a tornado that had swept through the week before.

I'd buried a father and daughter only yesterday, grateful my emotions seemed to be in a state of paralysis due to my current personal crisis. The funeral had been one of the hardest I'd done, watching a wife and mother put her world into the ground while she silently fell apart.

Time had moved differently over the past forty-eight hours. It was a blur, yet interminably long. But life kept moving around me, despite my desperation for everything to stop. There were still employees, families, and victims to deal with. Life and death were an unceasing circle, and if I could count on nothing else in this world, I could always count on the dead.

I padded down the stairs to the second-floor landing, where the carpet changed from threadbare to soft and plush beneath my feet. I always left the lights on at the front of the funeral home. There had been attempted break-ins a time or two through the years, usually kids thinking it would be cool to spend Halloween night inside with the bodies who temporarily lived here.

I'd thought the same when I was a teenager. We'd dress in our costumes and lie to our parents about where we were going—not that my parents cared one way or the other what I did with my time—and then Vaughn would sneak beer he'd stolen from his father and I'd let everyone inside with the extra key of the funeral home I'd filched from my parents.

Jack and Dickie would bring snacks and we'd tell stories and scare ourselves to death, never lasting all the way through the night before we ended up back at the Lawsons' and the security of knowing no one was going to murder us in our sleep. It was a bitter-sweet memory. Most of my memories involved Jack.

I quickened my steps to outrun my thoughts and tied the belt of my robe a little tighter. If my brain couldn't be bothered with sleep, at least it could be bothered with work. I figured I'd eventually exhaust myself and I'd have no choice but to sleep.

I veered away from the viewing rooms and offices and headed toward the side of the large Colonial that was reserved for employee use. I flipped on the kitchen lights and squinted against the brightness, and then I moved automatically to the coffee maker.

Making lists was my way of keeping it together— whether it was mentally naming the muscles in the body, writing a grocery list, or organizing everything in my desk drawers—organization was my coping mechanism. I knew with my depression it was good to make plans for the future. Not ten years from now, but ten minutes and ten hours from now. It was the little accomplishments that would get me through this. I'd been getting through things alone my whole life. I could do it now.

There were no embalmings and no autopsies waiting for me, though I'd gotten word that Lucinda Marks was on hospice and that I should expect a call to come get her within the next few days.

I'd signed off on payroll the day before, so there was nothing left to do on the bookkeeping end of things. I had a ten o'clock funeral to prepare for, but I'd already checked the details—flowers and pallbearers and the church arrangements were already taken care of. It would be at St. Paul's, and the burial would be on-site in the church cemetery. If the incoming rain would hold off for just a little while, it would make life easier for everyone involved. But I wasn't holding out much hope. I felt like I'd had a black raincloud hovering over me for the last two days.

I had another viewing later in the evening, and my weekend was booked with the last of the tornado victims. Staying at the funeral home made sense with my schedule as hectic as it had been. And if I worked myself to the bone, I might finally get some rest.

I'd turned my cell phone off a couple of days before, when the reporters had filled up my voicemail and their messages had gone from pleading to whiny to threatening. I wasn't even sure where my cell phone was at the moment. But if anyone needed to reach me, they could do it through the main line of the funeral home.

I felt bad about pushing the task of being my bulldog and keeping the wolves at bay onto Emmy Lu, but she could hold her own against anyone. A few bolder reporters had tried pushing their way into the funeral home, but there were laws that protect the dead, even against freedom of the press, and a few of the reporters needed reminding that I had arresting powers as coroner. At least for a little while. I'd not managed to get more than a sentence of my resignation written. I wasn't sure why it needed to be longer than a sentence, but it seemed after everything I'd put into the job that it deserved more.

Married life was hard, but it was even harder in the spotlight. Jack had a high-profile job with a lot of stress attached, and I had become more high profile over the last couple of years due to the victims we'd served. Living life in the fishbowl wasn't always good. The situation we were in now was a perfect example. I didn't need our lives and the details of our marriage splashed across the front page—both true and untrue. One of us needed a normal life if things were going to work between us. We'd burn ourselves out if we kept going the direction we were going.

Jack was called to lead. My position could easily be sacrificed. And maybe if I resigned we could have normal conversations that didn't revolve around death, or find our innermost secrets shared with the world.

My routine had been consistent the last two days. When the staff left to go home in the afternoon, I locked the doors behind them, set the alarm, and sequestered myself in my office. I kept the phone off the hook and ignored the occasional knock on the door or ring of the bell. If there was a body to collect, the answering service would take the call and get hold of my assistant, Sheldon Durkus.

I wasn't sure if my isolation was because I was afraid of the reporters, or because it might be Jack trying to reach me. And then I realized how stupid that was, because if Jack had really wanted to reach me, there would've been nothing to stand in his way.

I opened the fridge and picked up the creamer, sniffing it to make sure it was still good before I poured a small amount in my coffee cup. I always added my creamer and sugar first and then poured the coffee on top so I didn't have to dirty a spoon. And on the days when cream and sugar seemed like too much work, I drank it black. I wasn't necessarily picky about how caffeine got into my system, so long as it did.

I still had a few hours until my staff showed up, so that left me plenty of time to stand under the hot water in the shower in my office. Maybe with the heat from the coffee and the hot water, I could finally get warm.

My office was just off the kitchen, and I started to make my way in that direction when there was a sharp rap at the door. I jerked to a stop and hot coffee splashed over the rim of the cup and onto my hand. I stared at it, trying to get my brain to register the pain, even as my skin turned red.

My reactions were slow, but instinct took over. I reached into the drawer of the island and grabbed the small revolver, the plastic grip rough in my hand. And then I waited. There was another knock. This one less intense, and then I felt my heart stop as I heard Jack's voice.

"Jaye," he said. "I know you're in there. I saw the lights come on. I'm coming in."

I looked around frantically. I couldn't do this right now. I wasn't prepared to see him. I'd spent the last two days trying to figure out what I'd say to him if I ever saw him again, but I'd come up with nothing. There were no words to combat against the broken pieces of my heart.

I heard the key turning in the lock, and still I stood as if my feet were cemented to the floor. My heart-beat fluttered erratically at the base of my throat as the door opened and the alarm started beeping its warning before being quickly shut off. I needed to run. To hide. Not in fear. I could never fear Jack. But I hadn't realized until this week what marriage really meant—that there were pieces of yourself that belonged to the other and it was their job to shelter and protect those pieces. And when they didn't shelter and protect those most delicate parts of the heart and soul, the destruction left in their place seemed impossible to repair.

Tears stung my eyes and I blinked rapidly. I couldn't afford to let him see me cry. I hadn't been able to cry since I'd walked out of the house and away from the life I thought we were starting together.

I hadn't looked at myself in the mirror, and I didn't know what I looked like, but I knew for certain I wasn't at my best. After looking at Jack, it seemed I wasn't alone in that, though it was little consolation.

Jack had entered through the side door where we bring the bodies through, and I heard his footsteps as he came through the mudroom, each step filling me with dread. His face had haunted my dreams the past two nights, but the man who looked at me now seemed almost a stranger.

Jack was a big man—imposing—but he looked withered inside his frame. He hadn't shaved, but the beard didn't disguise the shadows in his face. Like me, he still wore his work clothes and they were slightly rumpled, so I knew he'd put in a long day. There were dark circles under his eyes, and when I finally found the courage to meet his gaze, I saw nothing but misery there.

He glanced down at my hand holding the revolver and said, "I guess I probably deserve that."

I'd forgotten I was holding it, and I quickly put it back in the drawer. I wasn't sure I had the voice to speak. I was trying to focus on breathing at the moment, so speaking seemed less important.

I don't know how long we stood there, staring at each other as if we'd never known the other. My emotions were all over the place. There was hurt, yes. But I also had pride and a great deal of anger. I could feel it rumbling beneath the surface. I rarely got angry—really and truly angry—but when I did it was usually with destructive words that could never be taken back. Hurt others before they could hurt me —the Graves family motto.

"Jaye," Jack finally said, his voice raspy. "I screwed up. And I'm sorry."

I'd imagined an apology would make me feel better, but it didn't. I could see the sincerity in his words, and even as angry and hurt as I was, I hated to see the pain he was carrying. But his apology barely penetrated my numbness.

"It's taken you two days to figure out that you screwed up?" I asked, my fists clenching. I shoved them in the pockets of my robe, but I knew he'd noticed. Jack noticed everything.

"I knew I'd screwed up the second I heard the front door close behind you," he said. "I should have stopped you, but I didn't. I was overwhelmed and needed some space, but I know space was probably the worst thing I could have given you. I kept telling myself I just needed to give myself a little more time to figure out what to do. But I was just holding off this meeting because I was embarrassed and ashamed and afraid."

"Afraid?" I asked. Fear wasn't something Jack normally dealt with. He was smart and calculating and he went into situations prepared and with eyes wide open.

"Afraid I screwed up so bad I'd lost you," he admitted.

I didn't say anything, and he pressed his lips together and nodded, understanding my silence for my own conflict as far as the future of our relationship.

"I know you weren't the one to go to the press about Lydia," he said. "I know you'd never betray me. But it's an old wound." He put his hands on his hips and let out a breath. "And if I'm being honest I guess it's an old wound that's never healed. Can I have some of that coffee? I haven't slept in a while."

I nodded and moved out of the way so I didn't have to cross his path. I didn't want the familiarity of his scent or accidental touch. I could only withstand against so much. I didn't watch him pour the coffee, but stood with my back to him, wishing I'd opened all the blinds so I could look out into the early morning darkness.

"When I read the story on the front page of the paper, I was blindsided," he said. "Everything that happened with Lydia." He stopped and sighed and I turned around just in time to see the anguish on his face. "It'd be stupid not to admit the whole situation didn't hurt. I've got a son somewhere out there I know nothing about and have never seen. Before you and I finally stopped dancing around and got together I would think about what my life would be like now if Lydia had chosen me and let me be a father. But I can't regret that. What she and I had burned hot and faded fast. And if we'd stayed together out of duty for a child, I'd never have known the gift of you."

He dropped his head and stared into the depths of his coffee. My heart broke for him. "I wanted to be a father," he admitted. And then he made a sound that was somewhere between a laugh and a sob. "I wasn't ready to be a father, but I wanted to be one. And over the years, I've tried to make myself forget. And at certain times, I did forget." He sighed and took a sip, giving himself a chance to get control. "I never told anyone but you. I'm not even sure why I told you. I had this thought that keeping it to myself was like a punishment, but now everybody knows."

"I never told anyone," I said, my throat dry.

"I know that," he said. "If I'd had a thought in my head when I read the headline and you hadn't been the closest target, common sense would have eventually prevailed. I'm sorry. And I'm asking you to forgive me. You are the most important person in my life, and the last two days have been hell. I don't care about the election or Floyd Parker or the fact that I've been dodging my mother for two days. I don't care that investors and lobbyists have been trying to bully their way into King George and the last person they want to win this election is me. I don't care how Floyd found out about Lydia or anything else I've done in my life. Nothing matters but you."

A single tear fell to my cheek, but I didn't wipe it away. My thoughts were all in a jumble, and though I understood everything Jack was saying, I'd retreated into protection mode. I couldn't trust myself or my decisions, and apologies and forgiveness didn't magically take away the hurt and brokenness I was feeling. It didn't take away the feeling that I was the one who'd been betrayed.

I cleared my throat and felt another tear hit my cheek. "Jack," I said. Even saying his name was difficult. "Believe it or not, I understand everything you're saying. I know you well. Or at least thought I did before two days ago. Now I'm not so sure. But I knew this was something you carried deep inside of you. I wished you'd felt comfortable sharing your feelings with me, but you had your reasons for staying quiet. I also understand the stress you've been under, whether you want to admit the election is getting to you or not."

It hurt to breathe, each inhale feeling like knives in my chest. "This matters. You're good at your job and the people in this county need you. And personally, I don't see what the big deal is about this breaking news. Sure, this is small-town Virginia with old Southern values, but everyone has skeletons in their closet. We could have handled this together, as a team, and everyone in town would've been talking about it because that's what they do. But they would've moved on eventually.

"I could even understand why your first thought was that I'd let something slip at some point in my life. It's a logical conclusion if you know you've never told that secret to another living soul." I finally reached up and wiped the tears from my cheeks. The more I talked, the more the anger that had been suppressed by the hurt wanted to surface. "What I can't understand is why you didn't believe me when I told you I didn't. We're supposed to believe in each other. Have each other's backs. Always. Right? I thought that's what marriage was. I was mistakenly under the impression that you trusted me. That if I told you to believe me and believe in me, that you would. No questions asked. Because that's how much I believe in you."

I ignored the tears in Jack's eyes. I had to or I would completely fall apart. "Do I forgive you?" I asked him. "Of course I do. I still love you. I still support you. I still believe in you. But I don't know who I am to you, Jack. I know I've always trusted you, but I don't know if I can trust you with my heart. I'd be lying if I said you didn't do some serious damage to me as a person. You have five days until the election. It's time to pull ourselves together and do damage control. But I need some time and space to think things through on a personal level. I'm too tired to make any rational decisions right now."

"Fair enough," Jack said. "But I'm not going to give up on us. I'll never stop coming for you. You're it for me, Jaye. And I'll give you your space, but I won't let you run and hide forever. I'd bring you back from the ends of the earth or follow you there if I had to."

His gaze was dark and intense, and he set down his coffee, barely touched. I wasn't surprised. I made terrible coffee. And he walked around the island and back toward the entrance of the mudroom. He stopped when he got there and turned back to face me.

"I know this isn't over yet," he said. "We've still got a lot to talk about and work through. But I'm just asking that you don't give up on me. The unwavering faith that you had in me, I'm asking that you don't lose that. I wish I could say that the hard part is over, but things could get harder."

I couldn't think that far ahead right now. My brain was fuzzy.

"Go back to bed," Jack said. "You're asleep on your feet."

I nodded, feeling like I could actually accomplish the task if I closed my eyes. "Stop dodging your mother," I said. "She just found out she has a grandchild from the media. You need to talk to her."

"I had to talk to you first," he said. "I'm going to see her next. I love you. And I need you. Not for an election or my pride or any reason other than the fact that it's always been you. You're my heart and soul. And I'm humbly putting them both in your hands."

With those parting words, he reset the alarm and then locked the door behind him when he left. I wasn't sure how long I stood in the kitchen, staring after him, trying to decide if he'd even been there at all or if I was just so desperate to see him my mind had conjured the whole thing.

I shook my head, trying to clear the cobwebs, and breathed in the lingering scent of him. He'd been real. And I had choices to make. I turned out the lights and shuffled out of the kitchen, making my way to my office. The couch beckoned me and I grabbed the plush blanket that hung over the back of my office chair and wrapped it around me before curling up on the couch. My eyes closed before my head hit the pillow.

2

I WOKE SUDDENLY AND WITH AN ALERTNESS THAT seemed odd considering my exhaustion. I looked toward the window and saw the gray clouds of an impending storm and no sun in sight. I hated doing funerals in the rain. The thought of the funeral had me panicking. I looked toward the clock on the wall and breathed out a sigh of relief. I hadn't slept through. It was just after eight in the morning.

"Wow, you must have ears like a bat," Emmy Lu said. My gaze went to the door that was cracked wide enough for Emmy Lu to stick her head in. "I barely made a sound when I turned the knob."

"Come on in," I told her, swinging my legs around so my feet touched the floor. I hadn't slept in the most comfortable position, and my body was protesting, but I was just thankful for what little sleep I'd had.

Emmy Lu had only been working for me for a short while, but it felt like she'd been there forever. She was so efficient and organized and loyal I wondered how I'd ever gotten anything done without her.

She was a decade or so older than I was, and she had that soft, round, motherly look that guaranteed no bull and great hugs. Her five boys could attest to that. She had a lot of hair that was always piled on the top of her head and seemed to grow larger as the day went on, and her cheeks were perpetually rosy.

"I'm sorry to disturb you," she said. "I know you need the rest, but a call came in from the sheriff's office."

Dread filled my stomach at the mention of the sheriff's office. It had only been a couple of hours since I'd seen Jack face to face, and his presence had stayed with me even in sleep. I'd dreamed of him, expecting to have him next to me when I woke up, so the disappointment of waking alone on the couch in my office brought things back into perspective.

"What happened?" I asked, stretching my neck from side to side.

"Dispatch tried to reach you on your cell phone, but you left it in the refrigerator," she said, holding it up. "I saw it this morning when I went to make a fresh pot of coffee. I charged it for you, and it still works."

"Yippee," I said, taking the phone from her.

She snorted a laugh and said, "Barbara Blanton finally called me on my cell so I could pass on the message. Of course, that's not all she wanted. That woman would've sold secrets to Hitler as long as she was the first to get to pass on the gossip. I finally had to pretend like I had bad reception and hung up on her. Why anyone would have made a gossip like her a dispatcher is beyond me."

"She's been there a million years," I said. "And you know how it works with county employees. It's impossible to get rid of them. Who died?"

"Looks like a cyclist got hit by a car out on County Road 36. Vehicular homicide. Looks like he's been out there a couple of hours, but it's a pretty deserted stretch of road so it took a while before someone drove by and saw him."

I grimaced. Cars could do a lot of damage to the human body. "I've got the funeral at ten."

"Got it covered," Emmy Lu said. "All the plans are in place and everything is set at the church. Sheldon and Lily will both be there."

Sheldon Durkus had been my assistant for the past few months. To give him credit, he'd jumped right in and hadn't quit after he was almost killed at a morticians' convention. He was taking his exams to get his license at the end of the month, and though his social skills left a lot to be desired, he was great at organization and embalming, so I was keeping my fingers crossed his awkwardness around the grieving would pass.

Lily Bennet was my pathology intern, at least until the semester ended and she graduated. I wasn't sure what I was going to do without her. She was brilliant, and she'd taken it upon herself to take Sheldon under her wing and get him out of his mother's basement so he could converse with the world. It had crossed my mind that Lily might be the perfect person to take my position as coroner if I resigned. Though the position itself didn't really have a lot going for it, so most sane people would run away from the offer as fast as they could.

"Okay," I said, realizing I couldn't put it off. "I'll get showered and head that way." I stood up and looked down at the phone. My screen was covered with missed messages and calls. I cleared the screen. I wasn't ready to delve into all that yet, so it was best to pretend it wasn't there.

"They said to hurry," she said. "The rain is holding off for now, but they don't know how long."

"Got it," I said. And then I cleared my throat and met her gaze. "Thank you for keeping things together the last couple of days. I couldn't have done it without you."

"Oh, honey," Emmy Lu said, coming over and wrapping her arms around me. "Of course you could have. But that's what a team does. We all take up the slack when one of us is down. You and Jack are going to get this figured out. Sometimes men do stupid things. They can't seem to help themselves. I've got to think the good Lord had himself a laugh when he created men and women so differently. It's any wonder the species survived without killing each other.

"You go on to that crime scene and show everyone what you're made of," she said. "All this nonsense now is nothing compared to what you've been through before. And remember that men aren't as tough as we are, not when it comes to issues of the heart. Jack's going to need you once he manages to get his foot out of his mouth. Remember what I said about teamwork. When one of you is down, the other takes up the slack. That's marriage, right?"

I was crying. I wasn't sure when I started, but the more she held on and stroked my back in nice, slow circles, the harder the tears fell. I didn't really know what parental hugs felt like, but all I could think of now was how much I'd missed out on in my childhood if they were anything like what Emmy Lu was giving me now.

"You give good hugs," I said, timidly putting my arms around her and hugging her back.

"Well, of course I do," she said, chuckling. "It just takes practice. You go on and get cleaned up and head out. Your bag and camera are on the hooks in the mudroom, and you've got fresh coveralls and boots in the back of the Suburban if you need them."

"I love you," I blurted out, and then immediately felt awkward. I wasn't sure I'd ever told anyone besides Jack that I loved them. But I did love her. Emmy Lu had babysat me as a kid and given me as much love and attention then as she did now.

"I love you too, sugar pie," she said. "Don't worry about a thing here. We're so organized things are practically running themselves. You go take care of this victim, and then you go take care of your marriage. It's all about priority."

She gave me a little wave and closed the door behind her. I padded into the bathroom and turned on the shower. She was right. I needed to decide on my priorities. Jack had screwed up. There was no question about that. But I could either wallow in his mistakes and my misery, or I could make the choice to heal and move forward. I couldn't imagine my life without Jack in it, and that was all the answer I needed.

———

KING GEORGE WAS a rural county with lots of farmland and national parks. The terrain was flat in some areas, more along the southern part of the county in King George Proper where the population was denser and where the naval station was located.

The more north you moved, the more the flatland turned to rolling hills and thick copses of trees. The houses were fewer and farther between, and the inconvenience of country living was outweighed by the clear skies and fresh air. The closer to the Potomac you got, the more the hills turned to rocky cliffs and towering pines that seemed to grow from the rocks. That was the area where Jack and I lived.

County Road 36 was about a twenty-minute drive from the funeral home. I'd showered and dressed quickly, and I felt somewhat refreshed. The clouds were moving across the sky quickly, and in the distance, I could see the storm moving straight for us. The temperature was hovering around forty degrees. It was the kind of day that deserved hot cocoa and fireplaces, not funerals and crime scenes. I'd chosen sturdy jeans, a thick black cable-knit sweater, and my rain boots.

I hadn't planned on messing with my makeup or hair, but Emmy Lu's words stuck in my head. I was going to show up with my head held high and let them see what I was made of. So I'd used concealer to hide the dark bruises under my eyes and brushed on blush to put color in my cheeks. There wasn't much I could do with my hair except to pull it back so it wasn't hanging in my face while I examined the body. It was getting too long. It was time to chop it off.

There was a cop car with flashing lights parked haphazardly and blocking the road where the accident had happened. Officer Plank leaned against the hood casually, checking his phone. He was still a rookie, and he'd clearly drawn the short straw. If the scowl on his cherubic face was anything to go by, he wasn't happy about being stuck on traffic duty instead of down at the crime scene.

He brightened some when he saw me, and I rolled down my window as I turned into the tight space he'd left in the road for official vehicles to get through. A few days before, we'd been in an armed robbery situation together, and moments like that tend to bond people. It also helped get some of the rookie shine off.

"Hey, Doc," he said, his ruddy cheeks deepening in color.

Poor kid. He was probably a worse poker player than I was, and that was saying a lot.

"Hey, Plank," I said. "I'm here for pickup. Anything I need to know?"

"I don't know," he said, his scowl moving back into place. "I've been stuck here. But I heard it was a hit-and-run. Don't know why a guy would be out riding this morning. The fog was real bad. I went on shift at six and it took me an extra twenty minutes to get to the station."

"Who knows," I said. "But I bet he wishes he'd slept in now."

Plank grimaced, and I realized he was still fresh enough from the academy to not appreciate gallows humor. I gave him a departing wave and drove past his car and onto the two-lane road.

There was barely a shoulder, and it definitely wasn't the safest road for a cyclist to ride, but even I could see the appeal as I accelerated up the first hill and saw the view. There was another cop car parked at the top of the next hill with lights flashing, and I carefully passed it, not sure what the scene would look like on the other side.

Cop cars were parked all over the road, most of them with their lights flashing, but there was an area cordoned off at the bottom of the hill where I could see the cyclist and what was left of his bike. There was an ambulance parked away from the police cars. They would've been dispatched with the initial 911 call.

I maneuvered around the cars until I reached the yellow crime scene tape and parked. It was obvious by the curious stares of the cops who'd cordoned off the area that they were surprised to see me. There were no secrets in small towns.

I remembered what Emmy Lu said about keeping my chin up, and I took a deep breath. When it had come out that my parents had been criminals wanted by the FBI, the looks I'd gotten from most cops and friends alike had been scornful or judgmental, as if they couldn't trust me around their handbags or the silver. The looks I was getting now were ones of pity. I think I preferred the former.

I knew all the cops on site, but there was one person missing. Jack wasn't on the scene, and I wondered if he'd done it on purpose to defuse the gossip and let me do my job. Or maybe he was putting out a million other fires and figured I could handle this one.

I got out of the Suburban and went to the back, opening the hatch, and I grabbed my medical bag and camera. I slung the bag across my shoulder and pulled out a pair of gloves, blowing into them before putting them on.

"Hey, Doc," Officer Chen said.

"Chen," I said, nodding. "How's it going?"

"Better than this guy," she said automatically. "What about you? Anything new and exciting happening in your life?"

My eyes snapped up and met hers, and I saw the humor and understanding there. I choked on a laugh and covered my mouth and added a few extra coughs so no one thought I was laughing over the victim.

"Same old, same old," I told her.

"That's a shame," she said. "People are assholes. Don't listen to the hype. None of us are worried about the election. The sheriff will win in a landslide."

I blew out a breath and said, "From your mouth to God's ears."

Kristi Chen had only been at the KGSO for a couple of years, but she was far from a rookie. She was a transplant from Atlanta, and she had a dozen years as a cop under her belt. Her size fooled many—she was petite and her uniforms had to be specially made because they didn't come in sizes small enough— but she had multiple black belts and I'd seen her bring grown men to their knees in tears during an arrest.

I found it curious that Chen was the only one who'd had the guts to speak to me. All the male cops had found something to do so they looked busy and wouldn't have to make eye contact. It was hard when a couple was fighting, especially in a work situation because there was an instinct to take sides. Jack's cops were and should be loyal to him. They all knew what would happen if someone like Floyd Parker was elected sheriff. Anyone with rank would be out of a job and everyone else would be miserable.

I lifted the crime scene tape and went under, and then I made my way toward the body.

"Who found the victim?" I asked, taking in the scene.

There was a mangled bicycle about two feet outside of the white stripe that designated the narrow shoulder of the road. Several yards from the bicycle was the body of a man.

He was wearing the proper gear—expensive from what I could tell—but even the best equipment couldn't provide the protection needed from a couple of tons of metal going at a high rate of speed.

"A motorist called it into 911 at 7:51 this morning," Chen said.

"Did they see who hit him?" I asked, taking some pictures of the position of the bicycle and the body at different angles.

"Nope," Chen said, rocking back on her thick-soled boots. "The lady that called was in hysterics. She's sitting over in the ambulance breathing into a bag."

"It's not every day you find a body on the side of the road," I said. And then I added, "At least not for most people."

That made Chen snort, and I almost started to relax, but I felt a shift in the atmosphere

and I knew Jack must had arrived. All the cops on scene went still, and though none of them looked like they were watching, I knew they were.

I figured the best way to get everyone moving again was to act like everything was normal, so I turned and watched Jack lift the yellow tape and come straight for me. He'd managed to catch a shower and change clothes, but he hadn't bothered shaving. I rarely saw Jack with a beard, but apparently he'd decided to keep it. He wore khakis with a lot of pockets and a chambray shirt with *King George County Sheriff's Office* stitched over the breast pocket. The shirt was tucked in tightly and he wore a black duty belt around his narrow waist with all his gear, and his badge was pinned over his heart. He hadn't bothered with a jacket.

"Sorry I'm late," he said. "I got caught up at the office."

"I just got here," I said. "Chen was filling me in. Victim is a Caucasian male. Has anyone touched him?"

"The EMTs checked him when they arrived and determined he was deceased right off," Chen said. "First cops on scene immediately secured the area, and no one has touched anything."

"Let's see if he's got some ID," Jack said. "You have extra gloves in your bag?"

I handed him a pair and his hand barely touched mine as he took them from my grasp. Just that small touch had felt like a thousand volts of electricity down my arm. I turned and moved toward the body quickly, trying to settle my nerves.

"Maybe his shirt pocket?" I asked. "There's a zipper pouch."

"He's probably got GU gels in there," Jack said, squatting down at the front of the bike. "I always kept mine in the front zipper pouch."

"Wait, what?" I asked, confused. "You always kept what in the front of what? I haven't seen you on a bicycle since we were thirteen."

Jack smiled and looked up at me, his eyes crinkling at the corners. "I used to cycle quite a bit before I became sheriff. That was before you moved back. Didn't have much time for it after I was elected, but I enjoyed it. There are a couple of local teams around here. This guy is a serious rider. His bike probably costs ten grand, maybe more. He's got all the equipment and riding gear."

"Holy cow," Chen said. "Ten grand for a bicycle?"

"Some are a lot more expensive than that," Jack said.

He unzipped the black bag attached to the handlebars and pulled out a phone and a wallet. Chen opened an evidence bag and Jack dropped the phone inside and then he flipped open the wallet.

"Brett Jorgenson," Jack said. "Age thirty-six. He's got a King George address. 833 Revolutionary Road. That's probably twenty miles from here." Jack looked through the wallet and then put it in the bag with the phone. "Credit cards and cash are still inside."

"There are no skid marks," I said, my gaze going to the top of the hill and then following the path down to where the body lay. "Coming off that hill, the driver was probably going at a pretty good clip."

"There are no skid marks anywhere," Chen said. "The driver didn't even put on his brakes after he hit the poor guy. He just kept going."

"The vic got thrown a good ways after impact," Jack said, his eyes narrowing as he studied the scene. I waited to hear what he had to say before I examined the body. Jack was brilliant when it came to seeing crime scenes. He could visualize himself there, in the moment, and it was fascinating to watch. "You're sure no one touched the bike or the body? EMTs didn't move it out of the way?"

"They said no, but I'll double-check," Chen said, walking off toward the EMTs.

"What's wrong?" I asked.

"I don't know," Jack said. "The victim fell to the inside of the road, and the bike looks like it was dragged a few yards down, but it's still on the shoulder. Something is just weird about it. If he was clipped from behind, the bike and the rider would be off the road, probably down in the ditch. You can see scrapes on the road where the bike was dragged."

"I haven't examined the body yet," I said. "But first impression is that it wasn't a direct impact. His clothes and helmet aren't overly disturbed. No signs of blood on the road or on the body."

"Martinez," Jack called out.

I hadn't noticed Martinez when I'd pulled up, but it made sense when I saw him coming toward us from the ditch.

"Hey, Doc," Martinez said, the surprise of seeing me evident in his voice. "Good to see you." He looked between me and Jack, trying to gauge the situation, but we both just stared at him.

"Find anything?" Jack asked.

"Nothing," he said. "No tire marks or tracks on or off the road."

"I want you and Chen to start taking measurements and reconstructing the scene. Something about the angles is off to me. Send me what you've got once you get it into the computer."

"Will do, boss," Martinez said, giving us a two-fingered salute before heading over to find Chen.

I knelt next to the victim and unclasped his chin strap, carefully removing the helmet and checking for any external wounds. Helmets were good. I liked helmets. Mostly because they held the brains together and kept me from having to hunt all over the highway for them. Not that I would use that for a sales pitch if I was a helmet company. But flesh and heavy machinery weren't compatible, and flesh always lost the battle.

I pulled away his facemask and noted the grayish coloring around his mouth, and then I closed his partially open eyes. They were cloudy with death, but there were no broken capillaries or abnormalities.

"You recognize him?" I asked. Not that I expected Jack to know all of the thirty thousand people who lived in the county, but I figured if Jack had been a cyclist at some point in his life than it had to be a pretty small circle of people. I'd occasionally seen riders out in groups with matching jerseys, but I'd never really given much thought as to how they organized.

"No," Jack said. "He doesn't look familiar. But I'm going to check with the cycling clubs here in King George. There's a good chance he's a member if he's skilled enough for this kind of equipment."

"He looks okay at first glance," I said, running my hands down his arms and legs. "Nothing visibly broken, but I'll see more once I get some x-rays. All in all, he doesn't look like a guy who's been hit by a car."

"Head trauma?" Jack asked.

I lifted the head carefully and felt for any lumps, but there was nothing. "Nothing outward. He's got to have bleeding on the brain or internal injuries. I need to get him back to the lab and start the autopsy."

"Do you think I should pull out of the race?" Jack asked, his voice barely a whisper.

We were both crouched over the body. I could feel eyes on us, so I kept my head down as I answered. "Because of a gossip column in the paper?" I asked. "Of course not. But if it's because you don't want to be sheriff then that choice is yours."

"Are you planning on resigning as coroner?" he asked.

My head jerked up and I met his gaze. "What makes you say that?" I asked.

"Because I know you," he said. "You're hurt, and you're working your way toward mad. You tend to burn things to the ground and make big changes when you're mad. So I figured somewhere in the back of your mind you've considered turning in a resignation letter."

I felt the heat in my cheeks. He was right. My anger was starting to replace the hurt. "You'd think for someone who knows me so well you'd know what I would or wouldn't do when it comes to blabbing your secrets to reporters or anyone else."

I stood up abruptly and walked back toward my Suburban. I needed to get out of there. Hurt and angry were never a good combination, and there'd be another front-page story on us if I stayed around too much longer.

I opened the rear hatch of the Suburban and felt the first fat drop of rain hit my shoulder. I pulled out the stretcher and a fresh body bag, and someone grabbed on to the back end of the stretcher and released the wheels so they touched the ground. It was Officer Wachowski, her face set in stoic lines as she helped me guide the gurney toward the body.

Jack had moved away, getting reports from some of the other officers and giving me some space. The thing about marriage was that I knew deep down we were going to be okay. That things would eventually work out. But there were a lot of emotions to wade through between now and then, and you couldn't rush the process of reconciliation. All in all, I felt like I was entitled to be mad for a little while.

We positioned the stretcher and then moved the body carefully into the bag as the droplets plinked against black plastic. Rigor had started to set in his face and fingers. There'd been a small amount of lividity on part of his face and neck where he'd landed on the ground, but it wasn't the deep purple of someone who'd been lying there an extended amount of time. But he'd been there for a while before someone found him. I looked down at my watch and calculated the time. He'd probably been dead three to four hours.

I zipped the bag, and Wachowski and I raised the stretcher together, and then we rolled it back under the crime scene tape and toward the Suburban.

"Thanks, Wachowski," I said once we had him loaded.

"Any time, Doc," she said. "We've got yours and the sheriff's backs. It'll all work out. You'll see."

I nodded mutely and felt the rushing in my ears. There was nothing left for me to do, so I tossed my things in the back and got in the Suburban just as the drops started to fall a little faster. I caught Jack's gaze as I turned on the ignition and the heater to full blast, and we stared at each other for several seconds before I put the car in drive and weaved my way through the labyrinth of patrol cars and back toward Bloody Mary and the funeral home.

It seemed Emmy Lu had opened the dam. I hadn't been able to cry for the last two days, and now it seemed like I could do nothing but. I wiped the tears from my face angrily and drove past Officer Plank without waving goodbye. And then I pressed down the accelerator on the open road and fled as fast as I could.

3

THUNDER RUMBLED OVERHEAD AND THE RAIN CAME in sheets that made it difficult to see. I called to let Emmy Lu know I was heading in with the body. Sheldon and Lucy were at the church overseeing the funeral and burial, so it would just be me and Emmy Lu to get the body inside.

I breathed out a sigh of relief and gave thanks for the rain when I saw there were no reporters camped out anywhere. I'd gotten used to them over the last couple of days, watching the comings and goings of the funeral home and sticking a mic in my face every time I ventured outside. Maybe they figured the story was over and the election was a done deal.

I parked under the carport and Emmy Lu came down the ramp. She was dressed Friday casual in jeans and a navy Graves Funeral Home polo, but she had a fleece jacket wrapped around her.

"I have to admit this is my least favorite part of this job," she said, coming around to the back of the Suburban. "I don't mind dealing with the grieving, but the bodies give me the heebie-jeebies."

Rain spatter bounced off the concrete and dampened the back of my jeans. "Which is ironic considering you work at a funeral home," I said. "Maybe it's because you watch all those horror movies."

She shrugged and we pulled out the gurney with Brett Jorgenson strapped on board.

"I like watching them," she said. "They make me feel good about myself. I can't imagine ever being in the kind of situation where I run from an axe-wielding maniac in high heels, or have sex in a haunted house for the thrill, or leave all my blinds open at night while a killer is on the loose. Compared to those morons I should be in Mensa."

I snorted a laugh and we rolled the body up the ramp and through the mudroom. I hung my bag and camera on the hook and then we rolled him into the kitchen. I typed the code on the keypad that was on the panel next to the door of my lab and immediately heard the snick that signaled it was open.

Cold air whooshed out as I opened the door wide and we rolled the gurney onto the elevator

"I'm going to get started on him," I said. "Anything I need to know?"

"Nothing worthwhile," Emmy Lu said. "A couple of reporters tried to nose their way in by pretending to need services for a loved one, but I can sniff out a reporter from twenty paces. I squirted them with the water bottle I use to water the plants and they ran off. I'll make sure you're undisturbed for the next couple of hours."

"Let me know if anyone from the sheriff's office calls," I said.

"You got it," she said, understanding in her eyes. She closed the outer door and it snicked as the lock slid into place.

I hit the red button and the elevator moved slowly to the bottom. I started to shiver as we touched down. I kept the temperature cold for obvious reasons, and it normally didn't bother me. But my body was in a state of shock, which was not conducive to making a good Y-cut.

I rolled the gurney to the far autopsy table, and then I moved to the Keurig to make a cup of coffee to help warm me up. I turned the thermostat up a few degrees and then grabbed my white lab coat off the back of my desk chair.

It was all routine, and routine was always comforting. I didn't mind the sterility of the lab—the white floors and walls, and the harsh lights that tinged everything in a slight greenish hue. I had three stainless-steel tables with drains for autopsies and embalmings. Thanks to my parents and the profits from their criminal activity, I had better equipment than most of the state labs.

I turned on the vents for air circulation and grabbed a pair of gloves from the box. I had an electronic pulley system to lift the victims from the gurney to the table, and I slid the strap beneath him, body bag and all, and secured him before hitting the switch and guiding him to the table.

From there I worked quickly, unzipping the bag and removing it carefully. I stared briefly into the face of Brett Jorgenson and wondered what kind of man he'd been. I thought of his family and how Jack was probably at that moment telling someone that their loved one wasn't coming home.

It helped to humanize the victims, to remember that they weren't just a body on the slab, and to do my best to give the living as much information as they needed. The victim would have been almost as pale in life as he was in death. There was a smattering of pale freckles across the bridge of his nose and cheeks, and his hair was reddish blond. He was young—a life snuffed out just as he started living.

I grabbed the other digital camera I kept on my desk and took another set of photos of every section of the body, and then I looked carefully at his clothes before I removed them. His gloves weren't scraped up, which meant he didn't have a chance to break his fall when he landed. In fact, the only scuff marks at all were minimal and on his left hip and thigh.

The table had a built-in scale, so once I'd removed all his clothes I notated his weight and height. And then I scanned his prints and loaded them into the computer so I could get a verification on his identity.

The DMV database didn't take long to pull his record, and my screen showed the picture of the man who was currently lying on my table.

"Tough break, Brett," I said. And then I turned on my recorder so I'd have backup notes to go with my written chart.

"Brett Jorgenson," I said. "Caucasian male, age thirty-six. Height is six foot two and weight is one hundred and seventy-three pounds. Identification verified through fingerprint match with the DMV."

I turned off the recorder and took more pictures, this time of the naked body, and again, I was struck by the lack of damage he'd sustained. There was slight lividity throughout his right side from head to toe and minimal abrasions that made the skin look raw on the outside of the knee.

I positioned the body and took a full set of x-rays, thinking I'd see the clear cause of death with splintered ribs or a fractured skull, but when I snapped the x-rays onto the light box above my desk, I saw nothing but a couple of remodeled fractures in the left wrist and tibia that were fairly old.

"Huh," I said, picking up my recorder and starting it again. "X-rays show no sign of breaks typically consistent with a hit-and-run. I'll search for internal bleeding and damage during the autopsy. Moving back to the victim, there are no visible tattoos or birthmarks, but there is an abdominal scar consistent with the removal of an appendix." I turned off the recorder and made the notations on his chart.

There was nothing unusual or spectacular about Brett Jorgenson. His lack of injury was uncommon, but everyone's body was different. His good health could have had a lot to do with the way he physically responded to the crash. He'd been at the wrong place at the wrong time, and now it was up to us to find out who'd ended his life early.

Jack, I corrected myself. It was up to Jack to figure out who'd ended Brett Jorgenson's life early. My place was in the lab.

I opened the drawer where I kept syringes and took several blood and urine samples for the tox reports. And then I washed the body thoroughly and made my Y-cut. I removed the lungs first, weighing them and taking samples

I'd been expecting perfection from his organs, especially as an athlete. But his lungs were scarred and showed signs of permanent damage. Whatever the victim was at this point in his life, he hadn't always been. His former life had left a mark internally—cocaine use if I had to guess—and I'd say that Jorgenson had cleaned up his act less than a decade ago. Organs immediately started to heal when smoking, drinking, or drug use stopped, but it could take as much as ten to fifteen years for the organs to function like someone who was clean.

I moved on to the heart and removed it, pulling the overhead light down so I could examine it carefully.

"And bingo," I said.

The heart was a mess. It was enlarged, and fluid and blood had filled the sacs. Vessels and arteries had burst to the point of almost being unrecognizable. The blob in my hand in no way resembled a heart.

"Massive heart attack," I said, grabbing my camera to take a couple of pictures.

That most definitely didn't go along with the vehicular homicide narrative. I wondered how Jack was going to feel about that. It was clear someone had hit our victim due to the damage of his bike, but the chances of the driver killing the victim were getting slimmer by the second.

I took samples of the heart and put it in a jar, and then I moved to the organs in the lower cavity. He had some scarring of the liver and there was evidence he'd been a heavy drinker at some point, but again, the signs of reversal were there, telling me that whoever he was now was not who he used to be.

That somehow made it all the more a shame for him to die as he had. I understood how hard it was to get locked into an identity and see no way out. It made me respect a man I'd never met to see how hard he'd worked to escape the choices he'd made early in his life. Addiction was never easy, but he'd overcome it.

I removed his stomach and examined the contents. There was no solid food, only water and something brown and sticky that smelled like chocolate, but the consistency was more like a melted tootsie roll. Probably something to give him energy as he biked.

What I hadn't found while examining each of his organs was internal bleeding or damage caused by the accident. I moved to the head and made a thin incision with my scalpel from behind his left ear, over the top of the head, and all the way to the other ear. And then I pulled the skin down over the face to expose the skull.

I took my saw from my prep table and turned it on, the high-pitched buzz always reminding me of the drill used during a root canal, and I carefully cut away a portion of the skull so the brain was exposed. I turned off the saw and then removed the brain in its entirety, turning it in my hands so I could see if from every angle.

There was no damage to the skull or the brain. Which meant Brett Jorgenson wasn't murdered. I turned on the recorder and said, "Official cause of death is sudden cardiac arrest."

That bit of information was certainly going to throw a wrench in the investigation.

4

THE BRETT JORGENSON CASE WAS TURNING OUT TO be more interesting than I'd originally thought. I'd been able to rule out vehicular homicide as cause of death, but the tox screen had left me with more questions than I had answers to.

It was obvious that the victim had prior drug and alcohol abuse issues, but there were no signs he was a current user. Which made the discovery of amphetamines in his system questionable. I couldn't rule homicide yet, because with a drug history, he very well could have been taking them. But if someone gave them to him without his knowledge and the result was a massive heart attack, then we were talking about murder.

The rain was still coming down in miserable waves with gusts of cold wind thrown in to make sure my rain gear wasn't as effective as it should have been. I texted Emmy Lu to let her know I was out in the field, and then I put the Suburban in reverse and backed out of the driveway.

It was after noon, and my stomach rumbled uncomfortably, reminding me I'd been living on coffee for the last couple of days. I was probably lucky I didn't have a hole in my stomach lining.

I crept my way down Catherine of Aragon, squinting so I could see the road in front of me through the wipers. I was trying to figure out where Jack was without actually having to call him. The scene on 36 would've been cleared by now, especially with the rain, and he'd had plenty of time to make the notifications to next of kin.

My best bet was that he was back at the station, which was good because I wasn't ready to be alone with him again. Crowds of people were great buffers for emotions. I stopped at the stop sign across from the town square—at least I thought it was the stop sign—and I moved through the intersection slowly, wishing I'd taken up Jack on the offer to put emergency lights on the Suburban.

I couldn't imagine too many people would be out driving around in this weather, so I took my chances and forged ahead. The usually crowded and bustling square was mostly empty of cars. The shops were open, but the doors that usually stood wide, inviting customers to drop in, were all closed.

All of the Halloween decorations had been removed from earlier in the week and now there were cornucopia and turkey banners hanging from each of the antique streetlights. There were soggy bales of hay and pumpkins displayed outside the courthouse, and in the patch of green space to the side of the courthouse were rows of scarecrows that each of the businesses in town sponsored and designed.

Another heavy gust of wind came through, pushing against the Suburban, and I watched as a couple of the scarecrows toppled over and skittered into the street. I made my way around the square until I reached the building where the sheriff's office was located. The county offices were on the left, the police department and jail was in the middle, and the fire department was on the right.

The parking spaces in front of the city offices were all empty, so I figured they'd decided to call it quits for the day or work from home. It didn't take much for them to close the offices. The fire department was supposed to move into their new firehouse at the end of the year, and when they did Jack had planned to use the space and renovate the sheriff's office and add onto the jail. It was a long time coming. The sheriff's office was so outdated it was laughable. Jack had been sheriff for four years, and he'd finally managed to pass a tax for the department so criminals weren't better equipped than the police department, and he'd been able to hire more qualified officers.

I noticed Jack's parking spot was empty, but all of the other spots were full, so I pulled into the mayor's spot. I was going to have to text Jack and see where he was. He needed to see the autopsy results.

I picked up my phone, deciding to text him instead of calling, when headlights glared into my driver's side mirror. I recognized Jack's Tahoe and he flashed his blue lights so I knew he saw me.

I tucked the manila envelope with my results under my rain jacket and tightened my hood. I'd already sent an electronic file to Jack, but I'd learned the hard way when I'd worked for a large city hospital to always keep a paper copy of everything.

I took a deep breath and flung open my door and jumped out into a giant puddle. Cold water splashed into the top of my boots and soaked my jeans above the knees.

I slammed the door closed and ran up the steps and to the front of the sheriff's office. I didn't wait for Jack but ran into the lobby. The heater was working overtime. To the point it was stifling, and I hurriedly unzipped my jacket and hung it on the umbrella stand by the door. I wiped my boots on the rug and made sure the autopsy report had come through unscathed. There were blowers set out to keep the floors dry, but they were fighting a losing battle.

I tugged at the collar of my sweater, thinking I might suffocate if the heater kept blowing as hard as it was.

I looked around the station and saw wilted cops everywhere—shirts unbuttoned or sleeves rolled up. The back windows were all open a crack to let in some air, but they couldn't be opened too wide because of the rain.

Sergeant Hill was manning the front desk. I didn't know him well as he hadn't grown up in King George County, but his wife worked at the bath and body shop just across the square, and I'd talked to her on several occasions while shopping. His skin was the color of burned caramel and he had darker freckles across the bridge of his nose and cheeks. His face was angular and his dark hair was cut close to the scalp.

"Why is it so hot in here?" I asked.

"The boiler is stuck," he said, sweat dripping off his face and plunking onto the papers in front of him. "Sheriff went to see if he could hunt down someone from maintenance."

"Ahh," I said, understanding. The maintenance offices were located next door. Jack probably had to track someone down at home to get them to come in.

The door opened behind me blowing in cold and rain, and I moved out of the way as Jack came inside. He tossed his Glowtex jacket next to mine on the rack and wiped his feet. His brow was furrowed and his irritation was obvious.

"Someone from maintenance should be here in ten

minutes," Jack said. "I had to call the mayor and half the council to get a fire lit. I finally told them if they were all going home for the day, then I was about to give the whole department the day off, and everyone could just fend for themselves. Who takes a day off because it's raining?"

"Thanks, Sheriff," Hill said, grinning. "I've never seen the squad room so anxious to be out on patrol."

"Yeah, I saw three squad cars parked over at the IHOP," he said. "I think they were patrolling the all-you-can-eat pancakes."

Hill snorted a laugh. "You've got a visitor, by the way."

I noticed the few remaining people in the squad room had all stopped what they were doing and turned to watch Jack's reaction. That in itself was enough to have me dreading whatever Hill was about to share.

"Who?" Jack asked.

"Floyd Parker came in about ten minutes ago," Hill said. "He said he's got some important information about that hit-and-run this morning. Looked white as a ghost. And he's got his lawyer with him."

Jack raised his brows. "That always makes things fun."

"No one took his statement?" I asked.

Hill shrugged and said, "He wouldn't give it to anyone but the sheriff. He was insistent on that. But between you and me and the fence post, I think Floyd hit that guy and he's trying to cover his tail. He was acting real strange. If you ask me, that's karma right there. And only a couple of days before the election."

"Maybe," Jack said. "But a man is still dead. Who's the lawyer?"

"Never seen him before. Not one of the locals. He was wearing a fancy suit so I figured he was from King George."

"Where is he?" Jack asked.

"Interrogation room A," Hill said. "I didn't figure you wanted him in your office."

"Good call," Jack said, and then he turned to me. "Want to sit in on this one?"

"Yeah," I said. "Actually, I do. But we need to talk about the autopsy results before we go in there."

"Why's that?" Jack asked.

"Because it's not vehicular homicide," I told him, handing over the file. "The victim had a massive heart attack due to a high dose of amphetamines in his system."

"A drug overdose?" he asked, surprised.

"I'm not sure," I said. "It's possible, but we need to rule out homicide. What are you going to do about Floyd?"

"We're going to let him talk," Jack said. "This information doesn't concern him. But sometimes people stick their foot in their mouth accidentally. Especially if they feel like they need an attorney with them. We'll just sit and listen to what he has to say. Who knows, maybe he'll hang himself."

We made our way through the squad room, and he passed off the autopsy findings to his secretary along the way. And then we went down the long narrow hallway that led to the interrogation rooms. There were only three of them, and they were small and dingy. Four people inside the room was going to be very crowded.

Jack turned to look at me before we went in. "Be nice," he said. "We might have just been given a gift."

"I can be nice," I said, baring my teeth.

"Right," Jack said, pressing his lips together.

He opened the thick gray door and moved into the small room, and I came in right behind him, closing the door behind me. Floyd looked like a bull sitting at the rectangular metal table. The chair was too short for his long legs and it looked like his knees were almost to his shoulders. He had the kind of neck that made it look like his head sat directly on top of his shoulders.

Floyd had played some college football and had been in great shape at one point, but all the muscle had started turning soft around his middle and chest, though he obviously still put some effort into his arms. He reminded me of a middle-aged frat boy, and it was obvious by the look on his face that he didn't want to be there any more than we did. His face was covered in a sheen of sweat and he'd stripped down to his undershirt.

Sitting next to him in another metal chair was a thin man in a gray suit. His square head was much too large for his body and he had a full head of thick dark hair he'd ruthlessly combed back from a wide forehead. He hadn't loosened his tie or taken off his jacket, and he looked miserable in his stubbornness.

"Sorry about the heat," Jack said. "The boiler is broken and maintenance is on the way. If you'd called we could have scheduled an appointment so we were all more comfortable."

"It's not a big deal," Floyd said.

Floyd's attorney cleared his throat and said, "I'd like it shown on the record that despite the inhumane treatment my client has received since arriving here, he's here willingly and with good intention."

"And like I said," Jack told him, "as of yet, your client chooses to be here, so there is no inhumane treatment to consider. Why don't you tell me why you're here, and then we can hash out the details. This is on the record. Why don't you both state your names and then Floyd can tell us why he felt he needed to come in with representation."

"Floyd Parker," Floyd said, looking around the room and spotting the camera in the corner.

Then Floyd's attorney spoke. "Geoff Mailer from Turner, Mailer, Thayer, and Cryer, representing Floyd Parker in this matter."

Jack nodded and said, "Why don't you tell us why you're here."

Floyd licked his lips and wiped his hands on his jeans. "I saw the report about the cyclist being hit on 36 when it came into the newspaper this morning. I think..." he said. "I think I might have been the one who hit him."

Jack didn't make any sudden movements. He just studied Floyd for a few seconds and then looked at the attorney. "I'm going to go ahead and read you your Miranda Rights for your protection and mine. It's standard procedure."

Floyd looked at his attorney and Mailer nodded sharply,

It didn't take long for Jack to run through the Miranda Rights, and then he stated for the record, "Also in attendance are Sheriff Jack Lawson and Dr.

J.J. Graves, coroner for King George County. Just run through your morning for me, Floyd. Tell me what happened."

"I left my house about six," he said, leaning back in his chair on two legs. "I have to do all my campaign stuff before I go into the office, and I'd just gotten a batch of the big campaign signs so I was going to put them out around town. I was driving my old pickup, because it has more room for the signs in the bed. The fog started to get real bad when I turned onto 36. I was heading toward the state park. There's a good place for signs there." He licked his lips again. "You don't realize the elevation on those hills, but when I got to the top the whole valley and all of the fields were covered with fog. It was so deep I think I would've been completely covered if I'd been standing at the bottom.

"I wasn't going that fast," he said, finally meeting Jack's gaze. He still hadn't looked at me, but I was fine with that. I wasn't sure I could've kept my expression blank. "Anyone who's been around here long knows it's stupid to drive normal in that kind of fog. I didn't see anything in front and I know I didn't hit anything head on. It was weird. I wasn't 100 percent sure I was driving in a straight line because I couldn't see the road, but something scraped the back end of my truck and then there was this grinding noise for a few seconds. I figured someone had dumped their trash on the side of the road and it just caught under my tires."

"What'd you do?" Jack asked.

"I made my rounds toward the national park and left a sign there, and then I looped back toward King George and left a sign at the library and another at the McDonald's off 301. I had to be at work at eight, so I went straight there. I didn't have time to go home and switch cars. I checked out the back of my truck, but there were only a few scratches and the corner of the bumper was just a little dented. I didn't think much of it until I got inside and heard the call go out on the scanner."

"You did the right thing by coming in to report this," Jack said.

"You seem surprised," Floyd said.

"I am," Jack said honestly. "It'd be easy enough to stay quiet and stay under the radar until an investigation played out, at least until after the election was over."

Floyd snorted out a half-hearted laugh. "So you guys could track me down and get the media attention you need to turn this election around by arresting me? I figured my odds were better at coming in and doing it on my terms."

"So let me get this straight," Jack said, leaning his arms on the table and bringing his face closer to Floyd's. "You didn't come in because it was the right thing to do. You came in because it was the lesser of two evils and would paint you in a better light?"

"Careful, Sheriff Lawson," Mailer said, making a note on his legal pad. "You're making unwarranted accusations."

"No I'm not," Jack said. "That was a question."

"Don't try and twist my words," Floyd said. "I'm here aren't I? No way in hell I was going to let you hunt me down and arrest me. Who knows what kind of treatment I'd get by the time all your 'buddies' got me to the jail."

"Now you're claiming you'd be treated unfairly?" Jack asked, his smile sharp.

"I'll remind you that this is all unfounded until it's been proven that my client was at the scene and it was his vehicle that hit the deceased," Mailer said. "My client came in voluntarily."

"We're not in a court of law, Mailer," Jack said. "The second your client admitted fault, even alleged, you knew an investigation would be opened. I've got no choice in the matter. I assume you're familiar with the law."

"It's not just a claim," Floyd said, stuck on Jack's question of fair treatment from the department. "You've been wanting to get something on me ever since I hooked up with your…" he finally looked at me then, his smile smug, and I felt tainted and shamed that I'd ever let him touch me, "…wife," he finally said. "If I hid this from you and you found me out, things would've been much worse and I'm sure you would've found as many trumped-up charges as you could against me. But I came in and confessed. The roads were foggy, and I never even realized I hit anyone. I'm still not sure. It's all just a terrible accident."

Jack waited until Floyd was finished and looking way too smug before he answered him. "Well, Floyd," Jack said. "Here's the thing about being sheriff that you might want to think about. It helps to actually know the law. I'm surprised your attorney didn't tell you that."

Jack arched a brow at Mailer, and I wondered what Floyd or his attorney were hoping to accomplish with this meeting. The only thing I knew with certainty was that Floyd couldn't be trusted, and that he always had a game plan. I just wasn't sure what it was.

"So here's what we're going to do," Jack said, pulling out his phone and sending a quick text. I couldn't see who he was sending it to or what it said. "I'm going to get a warrant for your vehicle, as well as a drug and alcohol test, and we're going to see if the damage and paint samples match."

There was a knock at the door and Cole stuck his head in. He took in the room quickly, and then his gaze went back to Jack. "What do you need, boss?"

"We need to get a warrant for Floyd's truck," Jack said, and then he looked at Floyd. "Is it parked here?"

I watched Floyd carefully and noticed the color rise in his neck, but he didn't move a muscle.

"It's parked at the courthouse," Floyd said. "It's the white GMC."

"Once you've got the warrant," Jack said, "we'll need to match it to the bicycle and paint scrapings found at the scene this morning."

There was barely a flicker of surprise in Cole's expression. "I'll head over to the courthouse now," he said.

"Get a second warrant for a blood and alcohol test," Jack said.

"I'm sure I don't have to remind you that I'll need to look the documents over before you can proceed," Mailer said.

"Sure," Jack said.

"Hey, I'm here to cooperate," Floyd said, holding up his hands in surrender. His smile was cocky, and I wouldn't have minded if I got the chance to punch him in the nose again. "You do whatever you have to do so this can all get cleared up."

"Floyd," Mailer warned.

"You're a real upstanding citizen," Jack said. "I'm sure the media is ready to report quite a story on your behalf.

Floyd shrugged. "Maybe. It's all about the headlines these days. You guys know that." He smiled again and I gritted my teeth so hard I saw spots dancing in front of my eyes.

"Let's get back to the law," Jack said.

Floyd smiled again and his eyes went mean. "You can keep telling me about the law, but we both know it's the court of popular opinion that really matters at times like this. You had your chance to bring King George to the next level. You could have been awarded a billion-dollar contract to bring the federal prisons here. I would've created jobs and lined everyone's pockets nicely."

"And I've told you and anyone else who asks time and time again that I'm not putting farmers out of business and bringing the worst of the worst criminals to our county just to line a few people's pockets." Jack narrowed his eyes, and whatever Floyd saw in them made him shrink back in his chair. "I know that's why you were hooked up with John Donnelly and big donors like Mike Costello. But whatever your plan is—and I'm sure you think you have one—it seems your attorney should've advised you somewhat about the law."

"We both know that any frivolous charges you bring against my client will be tossed out," Mailer said. "There's no reason to waste the taxpayers' money or any of our time."

"Here's the thing, Mailer," Jack said, his dark eyes like lasers as he pinned the man down. "A man died. So I don't consider his life to be a waste of taxpayer money or my time. What you're doing is gambling. You and Floyd worked out a scheme to come in and confess, thinking I'd worry more about my reputation and how I'd look than the victim. I don't consider any charges frivolous at this point. And I'm sure we'll have a definite cause of death within the next twenty-four hours."

I kept my face blank, so I didn't give anything away. I didn't know what Floyd's endgame was, but he'd put himself in the hot seat, so to speak, and Jack wasn't obligated to tell him the truth if it meant Floyd might incriminate himself.

"I'll expect a copy of the autopsy report," Mailer said, looking at me.

"I'm sure the sheriff will see you receive a copy," I said. I didn't report to Mailer, and I had no plans of gathering information for him like I was his secretary.

"Here's the thing about the law," Jack said, ignoring Mailer's request. "There's a difference between the letter of the law versus the spirit of the law, so let me lay this out for you. If we find a match on your vehicle to the bicycle that was hit this morning, you could be looking at something as serious as vehicular homicide."

Floyd scoffed. "Come on, Jack. It was an accident."

"There's no point in speculating charges when it's not up to you whether or not he'll be prosecuted," Mailer said.

"But we can still file the charges and make an arrest," Jack said. "An investigation has to be conducted. There's no way around that, accident or not. And someone died. That's kind of a big deal where I'm standing. Make no doubt about it, we can arrest you and charge you, and your attorney knows it."

Floyd looked at Mailer, and Mailer just shook his head and waved his hand as if he had nothing to worry about.

"Then there's the other charges," Jack continued. "You left the scene of an accident. Then there's a charge of failing to render aid. And don't forget reckless driving and crossing the fog line. Failure to yield to a cyclist would be another. And I'm sure a couple more will pop up once we start going through your truck."

"You're bluffing," Floyd said. "You start piling charges on me and you're going to look like a sore loser."

Jack shrugged. "I don't think so. I believe in the law and I always have. I believe without it things would be chaos. If you don't like a law, then work to get the law changed. But as long as it's the law it should be followed. So here's my question to you, Floyd, now that you've gotten a crash course on what the law entails as far as your stupidity goes. What kind of sheriff would you be? If it was me sitting in your place, would you follow the letter of the law? Or would you show compassion and mercy for a horrible accident, and show discretion for the spirit of the law? You've got the power to do either. What would you do if it was me?"

Jack's voice had gotten very soft and the color drained from Floyd's face. He'd seriously miscalculated the election chess game he was playing.

"That's what I thought," Jack. "We're going to go get those warrants. You started this ball rolling, and even if I wanted to look the other way, hell, even if it was my own mother, I'd still have to do exactly what I'm doing. The best thing to do is let this play out. My cops are good at their jobs. J.J. can draw your blood and get the urine sample once we have the warrant in hand."

"She's not touching me with a needle," Floyd said, shaking his head.

"Considering my client's past with the doctor in question, I consider that a threat meant to incite my client."

"You're not from around here, are you, Mailer?" Jack asked. There was no humor in his smile.

I wasn't sure I could trust myself with anything sharp around Floyd, so I was kind of on the attorney's side with that one.

"I'm sure we could find someone to eventually come in and get it done," Jack said. "But you know how slow things move around here. And you've got to figure the longer you sit here, the worse the gossip will be."

"You'd like that wouldn't you?" Floyd asked.

"No," Jack said. "I wouldn't. But while you're seeing this as a personal attack against you, I'm seeing a man who isn't going to see his baby born next month."

"Fine," Floyd said. "She can do it. I'm all about cooperation. Just get it done so I can get out of here."

"That's the spirit," Jack said. He stood and then pulled out my chair so I could follow him out. "We'll be back with the warrants. I'll send someone in with a couple of bottles of water. You might want to loosen that tie a little, Mailer. You look like you're about to have a stroke."

Jack ushered me out of the room and closed the door behind us, and then he took me by the hand and led me down the hall.

"Look, there's Cole coming from the courthouse," Jack said. "I was hoping he'd take a little more time. I wouldn't mind them stewing in there for a little while. We're going to do this by the book."

"Except for the fact that Floyd didn't commit vehicular manslaughter," I said.

"No, but the other charges will stand," Jack said. "And that's what we're going to go on. You know how bureaucracy works. It'll be tomorrow afternoon before the attorney gets a copy of the autopsy. We could probably even stretch it to Monday if we wanted. Nothing ever gets done around here on the weekends."

"Are you doing this only to get back at Floyd?" I asked. "Or were you serious about charging your own mother?"

"Floyd started this when he came in and confessed to hitting the cyclist," Jack said. "He not only confessed, but he confessed on record with an attorney present. I literally have no choice but to proceed exactly the way things are going. It's just a bonus that we get to make his life a little more uncomfortable in the meantime. I don't care about the election."

I started to say something, but he stopped me by holding up a finger.

"I really don't," he said. "I figure the outcome is already determined, and it's up to the people. There's nothing I can do about it, so it's one less thing I can take off my plate to worry about. There are other things more important at the moment."

I broke eye contact with Jack—his gaze too intense —and watched Cole standing under the awning on the front steps of the courthouse, looking for a break in the weather so he could run across the street.

Jack was a straight arrow, and what he'd told Floyd was the truth. He did believe and respect the law. There were rarely shades of gray with Jack. Right was right, and wrong was wrong. So if he told me he had no other choice but to do exactly what he was doing, then I believed him. He'd never compromise his integrity or the badge he so proudly stood for.

From where I stood, Floyd was in deep trouble. And if he'd had even an inkling of what would be waiting for him after his noble confession, he'd have known to keep his fat trap shut.

5

DETECTIVE COLE WAS ONE OF THOSE GUYS WHO everyone liked. He was a man's man, and could go fishing one day and be perfectly comfortable picking out lingerie for a girlfriend in a Victoria's Secret the next.

He had a slow Southern drawl and a smile that took forever to spread across his face. His Wranglers weren't a fashion statement but a way of life, and his boots were well worn. He was tall and lanky, and he wore a down vest over his denim shirt that was probably holding ten pounds of water.

Jack and I moved to the side as he finally decided to bite the bullet and sprint across the street. Cole came into the sheriff's office with a burst of wind and water, and he shook himself like a dog.

Hill tossed him a towel to dry off with, and then he waited until Cole was drying his face before he said,

"Whoops, wrong towel. That's the one Jenkins just used to clean up vomit from the drunk and disorderly that was brought in this morning."

"Hilarious," Cole said, tossing the towel back at Hill. "I just want to make it known that the only reason I'm not complaining about being soaked to the skin is because these warrants are for Floyd Parker."

Cole said it loud enough that everyone in the squad room stopped what they were doing to listen. Even Jack's secretary, Betsy Clement, stood up behind her desk so her five-foot frame didn't miss a single detail.

"So it's true then?" Hill asked. "He did hit that guy this morning?"

"That's what the warrants are for," Jack said.

Floyd had never been a friend to the police department, and his articles often incited issues rather than brought the community together with all the good the cops did in this county.

"Y'all, don't get too excited," Jack said. "We're going to treat this just like any other case. Take your time and be thorough." Jack raised his voice so everyone could hear. "Anyone who doesn't have something pressing to work on can pitch in on this. Floyd voluntarily came here of his own free will and turned himself in for hitting Brett Jorgenson this morning. This isn't about the election or anything else. A man lost his life. That's what we need to focus on. We've got warrants to examine his truck and to do a blood draw. We'll see what's left of any evidence on the truck with this rain, but maybe we'll get lucky."

Jack turned back to Cole and said, "Grab Floyd's keys and pull the truck under the carport in the back. Pick a couple of the guys to go with you and offer to let Floyd and his attorney observe while you go through the truck. Wear your body cams. We want everything documented. Jaye is going to draw his blood and take it back to the lab for tox results."

Cole snorted out a laugh and looked at me, his eyes sparkling with laughter. "I bet he's got those tiny veins that are hard to find. You'll probably have to stick him seven or eight times."

I couldn't help but grin. I'd already had the same thought. "It has been a long time since I've taken blood from a live person."

Cole looked down at his soaked clothes and then back out to the street where Floyd's truck was parked. "I guess there's no point in changing anytime soon," he said with a sigh, and then he clapped Jack on the back. "But I'd stand out in a hurricane and get evidence if it kept Floyd Parker from being sheriff."

"Amen," someone called from the squad room.

"Look on the bright side," Jack said. "You wouldn't

have a hurricane to stand in and collect evidence if Floyd was sheriff, because after we get done with him today, the first thing he'll do is fire all of you."

Cole choked out a laugh. "Well, then. I guess we'd better get to work." He nodded to me and made his way down the hall, giving two sharp raps on interrogation room A before opening the door and stepping inside.

"You have your bag with you?" Jack asked.

I just stared at him for a few seconds. It was easy to fall into work mode and ignore all of the personal things between us. We could always talk about work. Duty and justice would take precedence. But I was struggling. I wasn't sure I'd ever felt the pull and tug between bringing justice to a victim versus my own selfish wants. The victim had always come first. But what I really wanted was to tell Jack to pass this off to someone else, grab him by the sleeve, and haul him somewhere so we could have the conversation we needed to have.

There were a lot of unknowns, and I had a lot of questions. How did Floyd really find out that Jack had fathered the child of a married woman? What effect was that news going to have on the race? Did Floyd have any other tricks up his sleeve? Was he manipulating us now with this hit-and-run fiasco? Was our future supposed to be in this community? And what if Jack wanted to have a relationship with his son now that everything had all come out in the open? There was fear inside me, and I couldn't exactly pinpoint which fear I had the most anxiety about.

"I've got to run to the lab and grab supplies," I said abruptly. I turned toward the doors before Jack could read too much into the expression on my face. I grabbed my jacket off the hook and zipped up and pulled the hood tight over my head, and then I pushed open the glass doors and into the wind.

The storm had intensified over the last hour. We didn't normally get these kinds of storms this late in the season, but there had been nothing normal about this year. The rain and wind bounced along the streets and stung my cheeks as I ran to the Suburban, and when I got the door open the wind caught it and slammed it backward, catching me in the shoulder hard enough I'd have a bruise. I was just glad it wasn't my face.

Everyone except us had hunkered down in their homes, so it didn't take me long to get to the funeral home, pack the supplies I needed, and get back to the sheriff's office. I noticed on my way back that Floyd's truck was no longer parked in front of the courthouse. I could've called Jack and had him open the gate to the parking lot behind the building where most of the emergency vehicles were located. I could have pulled under the covered area and come in the back, but it was faster to just park in the front. I wanted to get this over with.

When I got back inside, I hung up my jacket and Sergeant Hill tossed me a towel. I held it up by two fingers and stared at him. His lips twitched.

"It's clean," he said. "I was just kidding about the vomit towel. No one has thrown up in here all week." He knocked on wood, and I used the towel to wipe my face and soak up water from my jeans, but it didn't do a lot of good. I was thankful the boiler was broken and the heat was up, even as my teeth chattered and I flexed my hands to get some circulation going. We would all end up sick between the rain and cold outside and the heat and humidity inside the building.

Jack was talking to Betsy Clement, though I knew he saw me come in.

"Is he still in A?" I asked Hill.

Hill nodded. "He and the attorney both, roasting like pigs. Cole hasn't come in to get him yet, so you're good to go."

I nodded and made my way back down the hall. I didn't bother knocking, and I didn't close the door behind me. Instead I shoved the wedge under the door to hold it open.

"Go make sure they're not planting evidence on my truck," Floyd told his attorney.

"Don't you want a witness here to make sure she does everything aboveboard?" Mailer asked.

"I can handle her," he said. "Just go do your job out there."

Mailer didn't look convinced, and I tried to look innocent as he gave me a hard glare, took a tight grip on his briefcase, and squeezed past me and out the door.

I looked up at the camera and hoped to God that it was still recording.

Floyd smirked. "Don't tell me you don't want to be alone with me. You used to like that."

I ignored him and put my bag on the table, opening it up and pulling out a plastic box with all of the equipment I needed. I grabbed a syringe still wrapped in its package and several vials and laid them on the table, and then I grabbed a tourniquet and alcohol swabs. I also pulled out a plastic cup with a lid so he could give a urine sample.

"Put your arm on the table," I said, trying to get him in a good position so I didn't have to get too close. He complied and purposefully leaned his body in, but I stepped to the side so I could reach back in my bag. I pulled out a white towel and folded it so I could put it under his elbow, and then I used two fingers to look for a good vein, satisfied when I found one.

"Stay out of my light," I told him, wrapping the tourniquet just below his bicep. "I'd hate to have to do this more than once."

"I figured you'd tell me it's just a little prick," Floyd said.

"It most definitely is," I told him.

I felt the vein site again and then tore open the alcohol swab, using it to wipe down my hands, and then I put on my gloves. I opened the syringe and pulled off the top with my teeth, and then I tore open another alcohol pack and wiped the area in the crook of his arm.

I put my thumb on the vein and then leaned down. "Make a fist," I said. Once he did I made a quick stick, hitting my target. I attached the first vial and waited for it to fill, quickly removing it and attaching the next.

"Aren't you curious about how I found out about Jack's little bastard?" he asked.

I removed the next vial and then attached the last one, unsnapping the tourniquet as I did. "Not really," I answered. "It wasn't a secret."

He laughed at that. "Is that why you moved out?"

"I don't know what you're talking about," I said. "I know you have a habit of overlooking and disrespecting the dead in this county, but I take my job seriously. We lost a lot of citizens last week, and a lot of people are burying loved ones this week." I grabbed a cotton ball and placed it on top of the puncture site before slowly removing the needle. "Hold that," I said, referring to the cotton ball. I grabbed a Band-Aid and slapped it on. "You need to pee in that cup. I'll get these back to the lab and turned in to the sheriff."

"And how do I know you're not going to skew the tests?" he asked. "Make it look worse than it is?"

"You hit a man on a bicycle and left the scene and you're worried about me making it look worse than it is?" I asked, stupefied.

Cole stepped across the threshold and I could tell by the look on his face he'd heard what Floyd had said.

"I'll escort you to the bathroom so we can make sure that you're not the one skewing the tests," Cole said. "And then I'll escort you to your truck so you and your attorney can watch us comb over every inch. I hope you're not paying him too much. He seems like a real dud."

"You picked the wrong side," Floyd told him.

"Why? Because I didn't fall in line with you and your goons. Not everyone rolls over for money."

"They do eventually."

"I'm under the impression that you're not taking what's going on here very seriously. All we can do is conduct the investigation to the best of our ability." Cole's smile was harsh. "And then we hand everything over to the district attorney, and you'll have to deal with him. Word on the street is you and the DA aren't the best of friends. Didn't you accuse him of corruption not too long ago?"

The smirk on Floyd's face disappeared, and his eyes narrowed slightly. I packed up my stuff quickly and closed my bag, wanting to take a step back in case Floyd decided to use his tackling skills on Cole.

"Here's what I think," Cole said, his voice softer. "I think you think you're a master at chess, but you're barely adequate at checkers. You misplayed your hand this time. I think you've gotten cocky and didn't actually understand the ramifications of your noble confession. Here's what you don't understand and won't ever understand. The victim is our priority. Accidents happen to good people. They also happen to bad people. It's just the nature of things. But there's a legal responsibility, even when it's an accident. So we'll do our job here because we believe in what we do and we owe it to the victim. And how you'll pay for the accident will be up to the DA. Let me give you a tip—it's best not to piss off all of the people you'd have to work with in a public service position."

Floyd stood up and grabbed the plastic cup off the table. Cole was tall, but Floyd had him beat by a couple of inches.

"Enjoy your job while you have it," Floyd said. "When I'm sheriff you'll be the first to go."

"I wouldn't work for a douchebag like you if I was offered ten times my salary." Cole turned to me. "Have a great day, Doc."

"It's getting better by the minute," I told him. If I could have, I would've given Cole a big hug. "I'll meet you out front once he fills the jar, and I'll make the results a priority."

Cole led Floyd to the bathroom at the end of the hall, and I felt lighter of heart as I made my way back to the reception area. Jack was there waiting for me, and he looked quizzically at whatever expression was on my face.

"What's going on?" he asked.

"Cole deserves a raise," I told him.

"Most of the cops here do," he said. "You got what you needed?"

"Cole is supervising the urine sample as we speak." I handed Jack my bag and reached for my jacket. I noticed it wasn't as unbearably hot in the station and figured someone from maintenance had finally made their way in to get things fixed.

"Good," he said. "I'm going to wrap things up here in the next couple of hours, and then we need to go talk to Brett Jorgenson's wife. Floyd might not have killed him, but there's a possibility someone did."

6

I took a detour and drove through Taco Casa on the way back to the funeral home. My stomach would regret it after having nothing solid the last couple of days, but it would feel good in the moment. I'd take the consequences like a big girl later.

I'd noticed both Sheldon's and Lily's cars in the parking area, along with Emmy Lu's, so I was guessing they'd cleared everything with the morning funeral. I looked down at my watch and realized there'd be people coming in for a viewing in less than four hours, so they were all probably handling last-minute preparations.

But when I walked in, Lily and Emmy Lu were sitting at the island having lunch. It was a cozy scene, and both of their faces lit up the moment they saw me.

"Please tell me what I'm hearing is true," Emmy Lu said, hopping up to take my wet things and hang them up before I dripped all over the place. I hated to tell her, but unless I stripped down naked, I was going to make a mess.

"Did Floyd Parker really turn himself in for killing that cyclist this morning?" she asked. "I screamed into the phone the second my mother called me."

I'd forgotten that Emmy Lu's mother worked at the courthouse. She would've heard about the warrants almost as soon as they'd been granted.

Emmy Lu went to turn on the coffeepot, making everything she did look easy and efficient, and then she turned back to look at me. "You look like a drowned rat. Did you jump in a pool?"

My teeth started to chatter. "Rain gear doesn't work as well when the rain comes sideways. It's a mess out there. I don't recommend it. And yes, Floyd came and turned himself in for hitting the cyclist."

"It's all over town," Lily said, stabbing lettuce from her salad onto her fork. "I'm not even from here, and by the time we were wrapping up over at the church, I started to hear all the rumblings that something funny was going on at the sheriff's office. Lots of people thought maybe Floyd had come to do something spiteful like measure for curtains in Jack's office, but old Mrs. Meador said she was betting that Floyd and Jack were just going to fight it out right there in the town square. She said it'd be like the gladiators and she'd vote for whoever was still standing come Tuesday."

"Glad to know where she stands," I said dryly. "The old bat."

I put my soggy bag of tacos down on the island. A normal person probably would've felt guilty for eating a bag of tacos while sitting next to two women who were eating salads, but I mostly felt sad for them that they were missing out on tacos in favor of lettuce. I was going to take advantage of my good metabolism for as long as I could.

"You're dripping," Emmy Lu said, handing me a cup of coffee and then going back to her salad.

I looked down at my feet and saw the puddle gathering beneath me. "Sorry," I said. "I'm going to change clothes and run down to the lab so I can run the tox on this blood and urine sample. I'll be back in a second. Don't touch my tacos."

I was running low on clothes in my office, so I grabbed a black pair of leggings and dug around in the closet until I found a soft sweater in an ivory color. I remembered why I'd shoved it back there. I looked terrible in ivory. My skin was already so pale it washed me out completely. But beggars couldn't be choosers at this point.

I grabbed my clothes and then brought them down to the lab with me. I set up the analysis machine for the blood samples, and then used a separate test for the urine sample. I wasn't expecting anything to come back positive. Floyd wasn't a stupid man. But I'd been surprised by drug and alcohol tests before.

Once I got everything going I quickly changed clothes and wrapped a towel around my head. That was another problem with long hair. It was definitely time to cut it short again.

I headed back up to the kitchen, and Lily and Emmy Lu were still sitting at the island, their salads gone, but a big apple pie sat between the two of them. Now that I saw the pie I could appreciate their healthy lunch choice.

"Want some pie?" Emmy Lu asked, cutting a large slice and putting it on a paper plate.

"Am I breathing?" I asked.

I pulled up a stool and opened my bag of tacos. "So how'd it go this morning?" I asked Lily. "Any problems?"

Lily and Emmy Lu looked at each other, and then Emmy Lu ducked her head down and I saw her shoulders shaking with laughter.

"What happened?" I asked, narrowing my eyes at Lily.

"Nothing happened," she said quickly. "There's nothing to worry about. Promise. The funeral went off without a hitch, and we were able to do the burial before the rain started. The reception was in that little side room at the church, and I didn't think we'd ever get out of there once the rain started. Mrs. Meador found an extra bottle of communion wine, and I thought Reverend Thomas was going to have a heart attack when he saw her passing out shots. I've never seen anyone talk to a priest like that before."

"Mrs. Meador is old as dirt," Emmy Lu said. "My mother always said hell was probably terrified to get her. Hurry up and tell the rest of what happened. I'm about to burst."

"Well," Lily said, biting her bottom lip. "It was during the funeral service for Ms. Randolph, and I kept hearing this noise. I thought there were maybe some kittens or something trapped in the wall at the church. It was real distracting, and some of the mourners on the back row kept turning around."

Emmy Lu snorted out a laugh and silent tears were running down her cheeks as she rocked back and forth on the stool. She couldn't even put a bite of pie in her mouth.

"It was Sheldon," Lily said, her eyes full of compassion.

"What was he doing?" I asked.

"He was crying," she said, and her eyes got even bigger. "I thought it was a real uplifting service, but something must have triggered him because he was a slobbering mess by the time I pulled him out of the little storage closet and got him outside."

Emmy Lu started laughing harder and I thought she might pass out. "Emmy Lu, what's so funny? It's a little sad. I don't think he's been right ever since we got back from that morticians' convention."

I looked back at Lily, trying to decide if I needed to have Emmy Lu committed, and I noticed Lily's mouth was twitching in her attempts not to laugh.

"That's not the funny part," Lily said. "I thought it would do him some good to get some fresh air and walk around a little bit, but I didn't realize his eyes were so swollen."

"Oh no," I said.

"Oh yes," she answered. "We had the grave site all set up with the tent and the grave was roped off, but Sheldon couldn't really see where he was going and he hit the tent pole straight on and then tripped over the little concrete divider. He caught himself on the podium, only he caught himself with his face. I think he's going to have a couple of black eyes." She winced, but I hadn't been able to do anything but stare at her with my mouth hanging open.

"Please tell me no one saw this," I said, closing my eyes. "We'll be known as the funeral home for clowns. I've buried a professional clown before. Their shoes don't fit in the casket."

"No one saw," she said hurriedly. "But that's not all."

"I'm not sure it can get worse," I said.

"Oh, it can," Emmy Lu said, wiping her eyes and making a strange wheezing noise as she tried to catch her breath.

"I don't know what happened," Lily said. "But next thing I know Sheldon is going ass over teakettle into the grave."

"Oh God," I said, glad I was sitting down.

"Don't worry," she said. "No one saw that part either. But you know how muddy it's been, so it was real slick in there. Fortunately, the crew was there early for the burial, and one of the guys was able to get him out with the Bobcat before the service let out. Sheldon was a real mess. I put him in the back of the Suburban with a towel and told him to stay there until the funeral was over."

"Good thinking," I said. I looked down and noticed the empty taco wrappers. "Who ate my tacos?"

"You did," Lily said. "You just consumed all three while I was telling the story. I've never seen anything like it."

"Hmm," I said. "In that case I'll have my pie. Where is Sheldon now?"

"He's lying down in viewing room three with an ice pack on his face," she said. "We've got the memorial service tonight, but I'm thinking he might need to sit that one out too."

I winced. "He's going to need to be there," I said. "We've had a case come up, and I'm going to be in the field the rest of the day. Put some of the makeup we use on the bodies on him. If it can cover up bullet wounds it should be able to cover a couple of black eyes."

Lily's face lit. "That's a good idea. Poor Sheldon. It's like having a puppy around all the time. You never know what he's going to get into."

Emmy Lu had finally gotten control of herself. Her face was red and her hair looked like she'd stuck her finger in a light socket. She cleared her throat.

"Don't think you've sidestepped the whole Floyd Parker issue," Emmy Lu said. "Tell us what happened."

"It's sounds like you know more than I do," I said. "Though I didn't see Floyd measuring for curtains, and there are no plans for a brawl in the middle of the square that I've been made aware of."

"Bummer," Lily said. "I'd have paid to see that."

Emmy Lu nodded in agreement. "But he did come in and confess?"

"That's the tricky part," I said. "The victim this morning wasn't killed by a hit-and-run. He had a massive heart attack after taking a high volume of amphetamines. Floyd just happened to be driving by when the cyclist died."

"So he's not a murderer?" Lily asked, disappointment in her voice. "I bet he's murdered someone at some point. He's such a scuzz. He likes to intimidate women. I told him the next time he crowds me I'm going to shove my car key in the soft part of his throat."

"Floyd Parker and his brother are both bad news," Emmy Lu said. "Everyone from Bloody Mary knows it. It's the people in the other towns he's snowed with his charm. But I've always said there will come a day when they get their comeuppance."

"Who are you talking about?" Sheldon asked from the doorway.

We all jumped. None of us had seen him creep into the room.

"Good Lord," I heard Emmy Lu whisper.

"You have a towel on your head," he told me.

"Yes, thank you," I said, holding my tongue so I didn't call him Captain Obvious.

Lily had been right. Sheldon was a mess. Both of his eyes were black and his nose was swollen almost twice the size. Sheldon looked like the lovechild of the Pillsbury Doughboy and Bob's Big Boy. He was in his early twenties, but his sandy hair was thinning on top and he wore thick Coke-bottle glasses. He came up to my shoulders in height, and he wore a lot of shades of brown—beige pants, brown checkered shirt, brown bow tie.

"You need to keep ice on that nose," I told him. "Is it broken?"

"I don't think so," Sheldon said. "I came to get more ice." He shuffled to the refrigerator, but Emmy Lu got off her stool and shooed him away, taking his ice bag from him and filling it herself.

"Did you know that more than one and a half million people visit the emergency room with facial injuries each year?" Sheldon asked. "And the most common injury is a fractured nose. Because of the protu-berance."

"Fascinating," Emmy Lu said, handing him the ice pack.

He nodded seriously. "I've always thought so. Like when Dr. Graves punched Floyd Parker in the nose. It's an easy and effective target."

"I'm still sorry I missed that one," Emmy Lu said with a sigh.

Sheldon pulled up a stool and put the ice bag on his face. "I've always felt it's my calling to be a mortician. But I'll admit I'm going to miss my forays into the world of crime. I can only assume that Floyd will let you go from the position."

Emmy Lu, not so subtly, elbowed him in the ribs, and he blinked at her owlishly. "What was that for?"

"For thinking that Jack could lose to a numbskull like Floyd," she said. "You're lucky I don't toss you back in that grave."

Sheldon took off his glasses so he could move the ice higher. "The probability of coming back from a scandal to win an election is—"

"Is extraordinarily high," Lily said. "Politicians are nothing but one scandal after the next. Nobody cares. So Jack has a kid somewhere. It could happen to anyone."

"Three point seven percent of men in this country have fathered a child they don't know about," Sheldon said.

"Well, there you go," Emmy Lu said. "It is what it is. I think more people than we know have seen through Floyd's schemes over the years, and they'll let him know just how they feel in the voting booth next week."

"If it's not a big deal then why did Dr. Graves move out?" Sheldon asked, oblivious.

Emmy Lu elbowed him again.

"What?" he asked, looking back and forth between the three of us. Emmy Lu and Lily got very quiet, and I took a bite of pie. "Are we not supposed to talk about that? I heard from my mother that you were completely blindsided by it. She said Jack might have children all over the place, and you'd better prepare yourself for him having to fork over his inheritance in child support."

"You need to tell your mama to get back on her medication," Emmy Lu said. My lips twitched and I shoved more pie into my mouth. "Besides, just before you walked in Doc was telling us about how Floyd confessed to hitting that cyclist this morning out on 36."

Sheldon blinked again behind his glasses. "There are almost 700,000 hit-and-run cases per year."

"So is Floyd going to be arrested?" Lily asked.

"I don't know," I said. "It's up to the DA. Since he didn't actually kill the victim he can't be charged with vehicular homicide, but he still left the scene of the accident and failed to render aid. Floyd and his attorney came in thinking they were going to waltz right in and out again, and the photo op and story the paper would run would show how cooperative Floyd was and how accidents happen to good people. Floyd figured Jack would let him go because it would make Jack look like he was holding a grudge if he arrested him right before the election. But Jack told him his attorney should've explained the law a little better to him, because it wasn't up to Jack whether an arrest was made. All he could do was gather all the evidence and hand it over to the DA."

"See," Emmy Lu said. "Karma. I bet Floyd is sweating bullets now."

"Or it's all part of his elaborate scheme," I said with a sigh.

"You give him too much credit," Emmy Lu said. "Jack runs a smart department. He'll charge him with everything from littering to jaywalking by the time he's done, if only to make Floyd's life a little more complicated."

"Jack's not that petty," I said, my mouth twitching. "Which is why it's probably good that he's the sheriff instead of me. Though I wouldn't put it past Cole to try to make Floyd's life miserable. They exchanged words at the end. Floyd made sure Cole knew he'd be the first one he fired."

"Ooh," Emmy Lu said, her eyes going bright. "That man is one tall drink of water. I would never go thirsty."

Lily turned an interesting shade of pink, making me think she more than agreed with the sentiment. There were close to fifteen years between hers and Cole's ages, but stranger things had happened.

"Why would you never go thirsty?" Sheldon asked, confused. "Two hundred and twenty-three people die a year because of dehydration. You should drink more water and lay off the coffee. We should throw out the coffee machine. You all drink too much."

"You throw out that coffee machine and you'll find yourself back in that grave permanently," Emmy Lu told him sweetly.

7

I WAS ALMOST RELIEVED WHEN I SAW THE RESULTS
of Floyd's tox results—negative on all counts.

There was something about Brett Jorgenson's death
that tugged at me. After I'd sent Jack Floyd's tox
results, I'd pulled Brett back out of the cooler and
looked at him again. The body told a story during
life and after death. And what Brett Jorgenson's
body told me was that he'd had a wild and careless
youth, but someone or something had gotten him
back on the right path. His body still had the scars of
that former life, but he'd worked hard to overcome
his past.

It didn't make sense to me that he'd do something so
reckless as to ingest that high of a dosage of amphetamines in his system. I looked again between his
toes and where his veins were most prominent.
There were no track marks or signs of doping. It's
not like he was on the Tour de France team. He'd

have no reason to dope. The whole thing was strange.

I looked at his file again and on the autopsy form next to the probable cause of death was a box asking about the manner of death. This was one of those cases that would've gone unnoticed in a bigger city and coroners who had a backlog of bodies waiting for them. It would've been easy to check natural causes or unknown, and turn him over to the family for burial. But I'd left the space blank. Brett Jorgenson deserved an answer.

It was just after four o'clock by the time I got a text from Jack saying he was coming by to pick me up. The funeral home was lit up like Christmas, and there were lights in the parking lot and along the sidewalks so those attending the viewing could see their way. We were expecting a large crowd for Stanley Turkus. He'd been a prominent businessman in King George before he'd been tossed about like a rag doll during the tornado. He'd thought he could outrun it in his car, but he'd ended up driving straight into its path.

Stanley had been cremated, so the family had set up a nice picture display along with his ashes at the front of viewing room one. It was the largest and could hold the most people, and they'd opted for coffee and cookies in the lobby so people could gather and remember the deceased.

The rain had lightened to a miserable drizzle, and I wasn't looking forward to getting back out in the elements. The temperature had dropped, so I went to the lost and found box we kept and dug out a cute purple plaid scarf and nice black leather gloves someone had left behind. And then I waited for Jack in the kitchen, nervously pacing back and forth.

"I thought you were leaving," Lily said, catching me by surprise when she came in.

She was dressed in tasteful black slacks and a black sweater. It would've looked absolutely ordinary on anyone else, but Lily was built like a pinup girl and she could've made a trash bag look stunning if she'd had a mind to.

"Jack's on the way," I told her. "How'd Sheldon turn out?"

She grimaced. "You know how you plan to do a little touch-up here and there, but before long it's kind of taken on a life of its own?"

"Yeah," I said.

"Let's just say that Sheldon has a strong resemblance to Barry Manilow. The makeup wasn't giving full coverage because the bruising and swelling was so bad, so I thought I'd try some putty. His nose expanded considerably, but at least all the bruises are covered."

"Noses are hard," I agreed. "I had a victim once who got his nose shot off completely and the family still wanted an open casket. I had to recreate the nose from a picture. But it was also an outdoor funeral in August, so you can imagine how that went once things started heating up and melting."

Lily snorted. "I guess things could be worse."

"Always," I assured her.

She moved to the coffeepot, and I envied how she managed to look like she was gliding in the stiletto heels she wore. She was close to six feet tall with them on. My feet would've been screaming within two seconds of trying to walk, but she made it seem effortless.

"Can I ask you a personal question?" she asked.

I thought about it for a minute. Most people I knew didn't bother to ask me personal questions. They just made assumptions or believed the gossip.

"As long as I can ask you one in return," I told her.

"That's fair," she said. "Are you happy with what you do here? Splitting your time between mortician and coroner? I'm supposed to graduate in December, and I've gotten a couple of nice offers working in the morgues at a couple of hospitals while I'm doing my graduate work. But being here these last months, I've gotten to see and experience another side of death that's outside of the lab. It's…I'm not sure the right word for it."

"Peaceful," I said, understanding what she meant.

She looked surprised and then nodded. "Yeah," she said. "Exactly. It's like when we're working a murder and there are autopsies and all this paperwork to fill out, it just seems so clinical. It's sometimes hard to see the people on the table as, well, people. But it's different when you're preparing them for burial. You get a glimpse into who they were. You meet their family. And you see how people grieve differently. I don't know, it's like there's sadness and despair on the coroner side of the job, but there's hope and resolve on the mortuary side of the job. One balances out the other pretty well."

"But you're worried that this is a unique situation and you couldn't do both," I said.

"Yeah, you don't really see a lot of coroner/morticians. I guess I'm just feeling pressure to pick one thing and see it through to the end. And now seems like the time to make the decision. I could go on and get my medical degree in pathology. Or I could stop now and go to mortuary school."

"Or you could do both," I told her. "You're twenty-two years old. Let me tell you from experience to get all the school stuff out of the way as early as you can. It just gets harder and more expensive the older you get. You are smart and gorgeous and kind and one of the most talented people I've ever gotten to work with. If you want to do what we do here, I know you'll succeed and I know you'll do it better than I could ever hope to."

Her smile lit up the room and she leapt toward me and grabbed me in a hug. I wasn't much of a hugger. I generally didn't like to be touched by random people, but twice today I'd had friends in my life hug me when I needed a hug the most.

"You're the best," she said, pulling back, excitement in her vivid blue eyes. "Don't worry about tonight. We've got it covered. And if Sheldon's face melts I'll lock him in the closet so he doesn't scare anyone."

She grabbed her coffee and turned to leave the kitchen.

"Aren't you forgetting something?" I asked, lips twitching as I saw the color appear in her cheeks.

"What's that?" she asked, eyes widening innocently.

"I get to ask you a personal question now," I said.

"Right. Shoot."

"Detective Cole," I said.

I'd learned something about getting information from people by watching Jack. A lot of times, the less you said, the more people felt compelled to talk.

I knew I was on the right track when her eyes widened and her face went scarlet.

"How'd you know?" she asked.

I just smiled and didn't say anything.

"It's not like it's been on for a long time or anything," she said. "Just a couple of weeks. I mean, we've kind of been dancing around each other the last few months, but he's never made a move or anything. He's always been a gentleman, unlike some of the other cops. But then we had that Judas serial killer and he stopped by to get information a couple of times, but you were out. And then one thing kind of led to another and we went out to dinner."

Her face was the color of a tomato now, and if I had to guess, they'd done a lot more than go out to dinner.

"We haven't told anyone though," she said. "We've barely been in the same room together during work hours."

To be honest, I thought she'd only had a crush on him. He was a good fifteen or more years older than her. So I was having a little trouble coming up with the right facial expression to let her know I wasn't completely shocked.

"It's the age difference, right?" she asked, continuing to fill the void of my silence. "I've always been more attracted to older guys. Guys my age are morons. They're too busy flipping their collars up and doing keg stands to think about being a good boyfriend. I want someone who has a job and is somewhat stable."

My lips twitched. "So you picked a cop?"

She laughed. "Well, he's hot too, and it's not very often I can find a guy I can talk about dead bodies with."

"That I understand completely," I said.

I liked Cole and he was a great friend, but like most cops, he didn't have the best reputation when it came to women. He'd definitely been around the block a time or two, and he had a tendency to start strong and then lose interest after a few months. But Lily was an adult, and maybe Cole would find something in her that made it worth giving the relationship a shot.

"Please don't tell anyone," she said.

"My lips are sealed."

"Thanks," she said. "I appreciate it. We'd just like a little time to enjoy ourselves before we start getting lectures about the age difference. He's kind of freaked out by it anyway." She looked over my shoulder and out the window. "Jack's here."

"I should only be a couple of hours, but if I'm not back by the time you're done then go ahead and lock up and set the alarm."

"You staying here again tonight?" she asked, her expression concerned.

"How about we each get one personal question within a twenty-four-hour period," I said.

"Fair enough," she said, saluting me with her coffee. "Have a good night."

I didn't think I'd need my medical bag, so I left it on the hook in the mudroom and grabbed the umbrella and my purse. Jack pulled up next to my Suburban under the carport, and I locked the door behind me before getting into the Tahoe.

He'd dried off and changed clothes since the last time I saw him, and his hair was still damp with the drizzle.

"What happened with Floyd?" I asked.

"We've impounded the vehicle for the time being and moved it to a secure facility, but we went ahead and released Floyd. I think he was almost disappointed. I'm sure he was planning to make a big stink about unfair treatment and election sabotage."

"You're not going to charge him?" I asked.

"I'm going to pass everything over to the DA, and it'll be up to him whether or not he decides to move forward. But I talked to him for a few minutes and he said he'd probably send it to a grand jury."

"Smart," I said. Sending it to a grand jury would keep Jack's hands clean through this. Floyd instigated the investigation. And instead of Jack having to make an arrest and look like a vindictive opponent, the DA would let the community decide on Floyd's fate. "It would've been nice for him to spend a night behind bars though."

"Floyd is due for some karma," Jack agreed. "I believe by the time we're done with all this a night behind bars will seem like a walk in the park. Remember the most important thing to Floyd is his ego. He likes being a big shot, and he likes throwing his weight around. The sheriff has the most free rein and really the most power in the county."

"Thanks to you," I said.

Most sheriff's departments didn't have to answer to the mayor or city council, but the last sheriff had been such a disaster that the mayor in Bloody Mary had very strategically moved in and taken control. Jack had spent the first two years of his term trying to undo all the messes that had been made before he'd gotten there, and he'd found a loophole that stated that one city couldn't have control over an elected county official. It wasn't fair to the people in the other towns that made up the county.

"Floyd has been biding his time over the years," Jack said. "He's corrupt, and I think we learned with our last case that most of his connections are corrupt too. He wasn't kidding when he said I'd pissed a lot of people off by not agreeing to building those federal prisons here. It's no coincidence that Floyd decided to run for office out of the blue. I'm sure investors were looking for a candidate to throw money at who hates me. We've got to do everything we can to keep him out of that position, or King George will never be the same."

I agreed with Jack, but I stayed silent. I wasn't sure what he and I could do at this point, though Emmy Lu had told me the cops had started putting boots on the ground to endorse Jack to the local businesses and they'd been handing out pamphlets off duty. Our best friend Vaughn was in charge of fundraising, and we had more donors and money than ever. We had ads and social media and commercials and billboards. It was the nature of the game. Jack's mother ran the campaign office, and all her wealthy friends at the country club used their influence. We had a lot of supporters, and we were going to owe every one of them our undying gratitude if we made it out of this mess still standing.

Jack turned onto one of the county roads, and I pulled down the visor as the setting sun was glaring through the gray clouds at just the right angle. It made the drizzle seem brighter somehow, like diamonds glittering on the windshield and the hood of the car.

"I called Mrs. Jorgenson and let her know we were coming back out to see her," Jack said. "Her family is coming in, but everyone lives out of state so they won't be here until morning."

"It must be hard being alone and get that kind of news," I said.

"She's got a three-year-old son to help keep her mind off things."

"And you said she's pregnant?" I asked.

"Yes, due next month. She has a strength about her. You'll like her."

The rest of the trip was made in silence. When we turned onto Revolutionary Road the sky was an amazing watercolor of pinks and purples and oranges mixed together on the horizon. The rain was still coming in a drizzle, but the clouds were passing quickly and it would be through before long.

"Wow," I said, as we pulled into the Jorgensons' driveway. "It's beautiful."

The Jorgensons lived on a good twenty acres of land, and the property was surrounded by a freshly painted white rail fence. A white farmhouse sat a good distance back from the road with a wide wraparound porch and black shutters. There was a swing set and play yard to one side, and on the other was a three-car garage that looked like it had living quarters above it.

The porch lights turned on just as Jack stopped the car, and I could see the silhouette of a woman standing at the screen door.

She opened the screen as we got closer. She was a pretty woman, maybe early thirties, with dark hair she wore in a thick braid over her shoulder. Her very pregnant stomach was hidden under a soft oversized gray sweatshirt and black leggings. Her face was plump from the last stages of pregnancy and it was ravaged with grief.

"Sheriff Lawson," she said, maneuvering her body out of the way so we could get by.

"I'm sorry to have to bother you again, Mrs. Jorgenson," Jack said.

"Marla, please," she said. "Honestly, I don't mind the distraction. It gets so quiet out here, and I was starting to get tired of hearing myself think."

She turned to look at me curiously, and I looked her over like a doctor looking at one of my patients. Her eyes were red and puffy, and her feet and ankles were severely swollen, but other than that, she looked like a woman who was in the uncomfortable last weeks of pregnancy who just found out her husband was dead.

"Marla," Jack said, nodding in agreement. "This is Dr. Graves. She's the coroner for King George County."

Recognition lit in her eyes and she nodded. "I thought you looked familiar," she said. "I used to practice law, so I was very interested in the findings of John Connelly's murder a couple of weeks ago."

I nodded, grateful she chose that case to comment on instead of our most recent mention in the paper.

"Why don't we sit down," I said. "You can put your feet up."

She choked out a laugh. "Yeah, I can't really see my feet anymore, but I know they're bad. My slippers don't fit."

I'd never really been around a lot of pregnant women, and even when I'd been working in the ER I rarely had occasion to treat one. They made me nervous—it was like waiting for a ticking time bomb to go off.

She led us around a small tricycle and what seemed like a mountain of toys scattered across the floor.

"Sorry about the mess," she said. "I've gotten to the point where I just scoot everything out of the way so I don't have to bend down. But I just couldn't find the energy today." Her voice hitched on a sob, and she nodded to the corner of the couch where a small boy slept. "I couldn't bear to put him to bed. I just wanted him with me tonight. Please, have a seat."

I did a quick glance around the house as I made my way to a straight-backed chair in the corner. Other than the toys on the floor, the house was extremely well kept. There were no dirty dishes on the counter or dust on shelves. The furniture was modern rustic, and the color scheme was whites and creams, accented with metal pipes and open shelving and a lot of shiplap. It seemed like a brave design for a family with small children.

"You said you wanted to talk to me about Brett's death," Marla said. "Did you find out anything about the driver who hit him?"

Nothing else she said could have told me that she wasn't from around here. If she had any connections at all she would've known Floyd turned himself in to the station already.

"Someone did come forward to say he thought he might have been the one to hit him," Jack said. "We've impounded his truck and we're comparing the damage. The fog was thick this morning."

"Brett always insisted on starting his ride right before sunrise," she said. "He liked to see the sun come over the hills. He said he thought it was as close to heaven as you could get here on earth." Her smile was sad and wistful. "It was just an accident. Brett was at the wrong place at the wrong time."

Jack looked at me, signaling it was my turn to take over. "Your husband wasn't killed by the hit-and-run," I told her. "Brett died from sudden cardiac arrest. His heart just gave out. It would have been very quick."

Her mouth dropped open in surprise. "How can that be? He's only thirty-six years old. Brett was in perfect health. He exercised and ate right. I have to hide the junk food in the house because he'll throw it out. Even his last physical came out perfect."

"Did he have a doctor here?" I asked.

"Yes," she said. "Umm…Dr. Wise in Newcastle."

"It would help me if you'd give permission to see his medical records from Dr. Wise."

"Sure," she said, curious. "Anything you need."

"I need to ask you about your husband's history," I told her.

She took in a deep breath and exhaled slowly, and she rubbed her stomach in slow circles. She'd managed to get her feet up on an ottoman and lean against the back of the couch.

"I imagine you would've found out a little about Brett's past during the autopsy," she said.

I raised a brow and looked at Jack. She was sharp, despite her fatigue.

"Brett had high traces of amphetamines in his system," I said. "They're known as greenies in sports."

Her head snapped up and her eyes flashed. "Brett was not on drugs," she said fiercely. "Believe me. I know what he's like on drugs. And I know what he's like without them. I would've known. And he never would've been able to function the way he did if he was using again."

"That's why I'm asking these questions," I told her. "The body tells a story. And what I learned about your husband was that he wasn't the same man he used to be. His lungs and heart showed signs of repair. There was scarring from what I'd assume was cocaine use. It never fully goes away, but our organs do repair over time. Same thing with his liver. There was slight scarring, but it was healthy. No signs of alcoholism. Which is why I found it suspect for that amount of drugs to be in his system. It was a large dose. Enough to work his heart so it couldn't keep up."

"You think someone gave drugs to Brett?" she asked, her face going so white I was worried she might pass out.

"That's what I'm trying to find out," I said. "The more you can tell me, the better we know what direction we need to go in."

She nodded and tried to sit up a little.

"Can I get you anything?" Jack asked.

"Not unless you can convince my doctor to induce early," she said, trying to smile.

"I was thinking more along the lines of water," he said. "But I'll see what I can do."

This made her give a short laugh and then she took another deep breath. "The baby keeps blocking my diaphragm. I feel like I haven't taken a good breath in weeks. He's already more than eight pounds."

"I'd be begging for induction too," I told her. "Just take your time."

She nodded and closed her eyes. "It's hard to even know where to start. Brett and I met our freshman year at Georgetown, but it seemed like we'd known each other forever. We were the classic opposites attract. I knew I wanted to be an attorney. I was focused on school and studying and getting into law school. And then there was Brett." She laughed then as the memory rolled over her.

"He was the perfect example of the college frat boy. He was a playboy and a partier, plain and simple. And he was the most brilliant person I'd ever met, even then. He made me crazy. He could party all night and ace every test without having to crack a book, while I'd spend hours studying. He was double majoring in math and finance, and he did an accelerated program to get his master's degree. I started law school the same year he started his PhD."

There was such sadness in her expression as she remembered, and I knew there was nothing easy about loving an addict.

"The drinking was constant while we were in college, but I ignored it. It's hard to tell someone something is bad for them when nothing changes. His grades didn't slip. There were no DWIs. I suspected he was using drugs too, but I'd never seen him do it. We were living together by the time I found his stash, and he'd been tapped to work for some hot-shot firm on Wall Street. Apparently, cocaine is Wall Street's drug of choice. They all use. It's like the adrenaline rush of the market and these extreme highs aren't enough. So they look for something that can take them higher.

"I thought once we got married he'd slow down a little, but Brett has always been ninety to nothing in everything he does. When I found the drugs in the house the first time I freaked out. I'd just passed the bar and we were supposed to be celebrating. But I kicked him out instead. You know how the cycle goes. He came back and promised to stop, so I let him come home. We had more money than we knew what to do with, and a good portion of that money was going up Brett's nose every month.

"Long story short," she said. "I got pregnant with our first child, and I'd had enough. I packed up my stuff and moved home to Connecticut with my parents. I was ready to file for divorce, and I was ready to fight to make sure he wasn't a part of our daughter's life until he went to rehab."

I looked at the child sleeping peacefully in the corner of the couch. His blue jumper had sailboats on it. "Daughter?" I asked.

She smiled softly. "Stillborn. I had my own issues to deal with then, and I still don't know why or how it happened, but Brett changed that day. It was a complete and total transformation. He never touched drugs or alcohol again. He was offered a job as an analyst at a competing firm on Wall Street and he took the job.

"So when I tell you I know he didn't put those drugs in his body, I mean it. When we were in college Brett's nickname was the Extreme. Everything he did was all the way. He was militant about what he put in his body. And he was the most regimented and organized person I know. He loved structure and a schedule."

"When did y'all move to King George County?" I asked.

"Right before Jasper was born," she said. "I didn't want to raise a child in the city. And Brett would have moved heaven and earth for me. When he got clean, he was the best husband and father you could imagine. If I told him I wanted out of the city, he would've done everything in his power and then some to make it happen. Brett is kind of irreplaceable at his firm. I'm not even sure what he does if I'm being honest. But he went to his boss and told him he was moving to the country and that he'd give him two days a week in the office and the rest at home. And they gave him what he wanted.

"I'd decided to stop practicing law when the baby came and focus on full-time motherhood, so I didn't have a job to worry about. And Brett was true to his word. He found this place through a friend of a friend and bought it outright, and we've been here ever since. Jasper just turned three. Brett flies into New York on Sunday night and he flies back on Tuesday night. Then he works from home the rest of the week." She stopped and said, "Flew," correcting herself to past tense. She wiped a tear from the corner of her eye, refusing to let it fall.

Jack had been right. I did like Marla Jorgenson. She'd been through more suffering and heartbreak than was fair for any one person to bear.

"Did Brett have any enemies?" Jack asked, taking over the questioning. "Anyone who'd want to hurt him? Any bad blood at the office?"

"No," she said. "Not that I know of. We're really isolated out here. It's what we wanted. I know his job was stressful. He didn't talk about it much. I'm not sure he could. I know he had to get government clearance when he started working at the new firm. But that's pretty much all I know. He didn't like to talk about work."

"How about the last twenty-four hours?" Jack asked. "You said he had a routine. Can you run us through it?"

Her lips were full and unpainted, and she quirked the corner of her mouth. "Like clockwork," she said. "He'd wake up at five fifteen when it's riding season."

"Riding season?" I asked.

"Basically, if the roads didn't have snow or ice, he was on that bike," she said. "The bike became his new addiction after he gave up the drugs. He'd ride every morning, weather permitting, and then he'd come back at seven thirty. Jasper and I would be up by then and we'd all have breakfast as a family. Then Brett would shower and get dressed and head to the office. He'd usually be done by four o'clock, and then he and Jasper would go out and play for a while to give me a little break. We'd have dinner together, and then on Wednesday and Thursday nights and Saturday mornings he'd ride with the club."

"Which club did he belong to?" Jack asked.

"Old Dominion," she said. "He said they took the sport more serious."

Jack nodded as if he knew what she was talking about. "He rode last night?"

"Yes," she said. "He got home about nine o'clock. I'd already put Jasper to bed, and I was so tired I went to bed too." She hiccupped and tried to control the sobs that wanted to escape. "I didn't say good night or good morning. I didn't tell him I loved him. When I woke up this morning his side of the bed was empty. I never imagined that he wouldn't be coming back home. I should have stayed up. I should have told him how much I love him."

I felt my own tears prick my eyes. I couldn't escape her pain. And it put things wildly in perspective. The moments we have could always be our last.

8
_____

THE DAY HAD TAKEN AN EMOTIONAL TOLL ON ME, even more so after leaving Marla Jorgenson and her sleeping son. It was a lot to process, and I couldn't help but think how I'd feel in her place. How I'd feel if when I'd walked out of the house two days ago, it would have been my last moment on this earth with Jack. It didn't sit well.

It was dark by the time we headed back toward town, but the rain had stopped and the moon was full in the sky. It was early yet, not quite dinner time, but the thought of food didn't sound good. I wanted sleep. But I also wanted to know how those amphetamines had gotten into Brett Jorgenson's system.

I breathed deeply as I snuggled back against the seat of the Tahoe, catching a whiff of Jack's Old Spice bodywash and the oil used to detail the leather of the SUV.

"Do you believe her?" I asked after a long stretch of silence. "About his drug use being a thing of the past?"

"I do," he said. "Everything she said rings true. But we can't rule her out yet. Maybe she's playing us. Maybe everything wasn't going as well as she wanted us to believe and she decided to make things easier for herself. We can't overlook his history. And we can't overlook her motive. I'll check and see what kind of life insurance or financial assets she's set to gain by his murder."

"Does that mean we're comfortable calling it murder?" I asked.

"I guess that's up to you," he said. "I can see how you could go either way. But you said you didn't find any recent evidence of drug use. If we take that and go by what his wife said about him being clean, then yeah, I think we need to find out how those drugs got into his system. And a spouse is the most probable candidate for being able to slip him drugs without his knowledge."

I could see the reasoning he was coming back around to. "Which means we need to look at Marla Jorgenson a little closer. Because he was just fine when he left his house this morning."

Jack let out a sigh. "Right."

Instead of heading back to Bloody Mary, Jack took the exit that led to King George Proper. There was plenty of traffic on the road for a Friday night.

"Where are we going?" I asked.

"We've got a basic idea of his schedule from his wife," Jack said. "And we know he rides Wednesdays, Thursdays, and Saturdays with his club. He worked from home, but she can't fill in his hours for us on the days he's in New York and the time he spends out riding. I figured we needed to start going to those sources who can give us a better picture of what he's like when he's not home."

I understood what Jack was saying, but I was confused as to why we were turning into the parking lot of Raines' Antiques and Vitamin Shoppe. Our friend Vaughn Raines owned the unusual, but popular, business. He'd bought the restored Victorian for a steal when the owners had gone bankrupt and had to liquidate. It was a huge three-story structure of pale yellow and a widow's walk. The porch spindles were painted olive green and the decorative trim was a dark rose. It was a monstrosity of a house and took up half the block. The parking lot took up the other half.

Vaughn came from money, so he'd been able to indulge his passion, which was antiques. Vaughn had also majored in business in college, so he was smart enough to know the antique store wouldn't be enough to be profitable, so the bottom floor of the

Victorian house was a vitamin and supplement store. Even I was blown away by the outrageous prices he charged, but I guessed health-conscious people didn't mind getting gouged.

"What does Vaughn have to do with Brett Jorgenson's timeline?" I asked.

"He's a member of the Old Dominion cycling club too," Jack said. "It's the same club I was a member of, so I know a lot of the guys who ride. We actually all started in the club together—me, Vaughn, Dickey, and Eddie. It's was Eddie's idea. His wife thought he needed to get out and get some exercise, so we decided to help him out."

Eddie had been married since right out of high school, and he was about as domesticated as you could get. He'd also always been on the soft side, and he'd been the kid who always had a note to sit out of PE. I couldn't imagine him exercising.

"Eddie was going to exercise?" I asked.

Jack's mouth twitched with humor. "He bought all the cycling gear and made it through half of our first ride before he decided to find another form of physical activity. Dickey made it a few weeks, but it was the social aspect he liked. And that's about the time he and Candy started dating, so he was…distracted.

"But Vaughn and I fell in love with it. It's great exercise and a great community of people. He's gotten very serious about it. He's invited me on a couple of trips to Italy that the experienced riders go on every year."

"Sounds like an expensive hobby," I said.

"It is," Jack agreed. "But if anyone knows anything about anyone in this group it'll be Vaughn. He's always an excellent source of information."

"Is that a nice way of saying he likes to gossip?" I asked.

Jack grinned and put the Tahoe in park. There were a few cars in the parking lot, but it was almost closing time. I wasn't sure how our group of misfit friends had managed to forge a bond since childhood. On the surface, we didn't have much in common. But when you looked deeper, we'd each been seeking family. Jack had been the only one of us who'd come from a stable home with parents who adored him. But he was an only child, and I guess in his own way he'd needed the kind of family we could give him.

I'd been the only girl in the group, but I wasn't sure any of them had ever seen me as a girl. Vaughn had tried to show some romantic interest when we were in high school, but he'd really been struggling with his own sexuality. We'd only gone out on a couple of very platonic dates before he'd told me he was gay. Since we'd all pretty much known that since third grade, none of us were very surprised.

A bell chimed when we opened the door and we

stepped onto creaking hardwood floors. The walls were lined with antique shelves and filled with colorful bottles of pills. There were pyramids of water bottles and giant jars of protein powder. Everything guaranteed to enhance your performance. That thought made me stumble.

"What?" Jack asked.

"Amphetamines are used to enhance your performance," I said. "Just like everything in here. You said you used to be part of the team. And you've always been involved in athletics. You never knew anyone to use steroids or illegal enhancements?"

"Sure," he said. "Especially when I was in college. They've really come down strict in recent years on the drug testing. But it hasn't always been that way. When I played baseball in college a couple of the guys used greenies. They ended up getting drafted to play for farm teams in the majors. It ended for them kind of like it ended for Barry Bonds and Mark McGwire."

"Okay," I said. "I can see taking them when you're an athlete at that level." I noticed the surprised look on his face and said, "I'm not saying it's right, but I can understand it. There's big pressure and big money involved. The competition is fierce for few positions, and there's always someone younger and hungrier coming up. But it literally makes zero sense for it to be the drug of choice in a recreational bike club. It's not like any of these guys are going to the Tour de France."

Jack snorted out a laugh.

We were standing in the middle of the store, and I looked around, wondering where Vaughn was. It was then I noticed the customers. None of them bothered to hide their curiosity as they stared outright at us. Even the guy behind the counter stared at us with rapt fascination. Jack nodded to each of them and even called hello to a couple of people he knew. It was an ingrained habit built from several years of politics.

I heard Vaughn's murmured voice as he came down from the second floor. He was talking to a woman in a full-length fur coat and blond hair twisted up like Grace Kelly. Vaughn came from money, and his parents had moved in socialite circles until they'd lost all their money and had to declare bankruptcy. Fortunately, Vaughn's trust had been untouchable since it had been left to him by his grandmother, but he was much more cautious and careful about money than his parents had been. But he'd still maintained some of those socialite relationships, and I guess they found it interesting that Vaughn had a real job.

I hadn't seen Vaughn in weeks. We'd texted on occasion, but life had been busy for everyone lately. In all honesty, he'd kind of isolated himself from us after he'd buried his lover last year. He wasn't the same. He never would be. Just like Marla Jorgenson would never be the same. The people we loved left a mark on us, and when they were taken, especially if they were taken tragically before their time, it scarred the soul of those who remained.

Vaughn looked surprised to see us. The surprise was immediately replaced by a look of concern. He gave the woman he was with a quick smile and excuse, kissed her hand, and came the rest of the way down the stairs.

He walked straight toward us and took each of us by the arm, ushering us to his office. The hushed whispers grew louder behind us before he closed the door.

"Well, if it isn't my two most infamous friends," he said, looking the both of us over. "You both look like hell." He pulled me into a hug and held me there, and I felt my body relax.

"You're the third good hug I've had today," I said. "I think it's a record."

"As long as mine was the best, darling," he said, kissing my forehead.

Vaughn had the polished looks of someone who belonged in the city. The people in King George were mostly blue collar, even though there was plenty of money to be found from the tobacco farmers in the area. There were times a millionaire and a farmhand could be standing side by side and you couldn't tell who was who.

But Vaughn always stood out in a crowd. He was as tall as Jack, and he wore his black hair long and usually gathered in a tail at the nape of his neck like it was tonight. His goatee was neatly groomed and he had a diamond stud in each ear. He wore fine woolen pants in charcoal and a three-button vest of the same material. His tie was silk and a shimmering silver, and his shirt was a thin pinstripe that looked like it had silver thread running through it, so it shimmered if the light hit it just right.

If anyone knew how Jack and I were feeling at the moment, it was Vaughn. He'd faced the same kind of scrutiny and gossip when people had found out he was gay. And he'd faced it again when his relationship with the priest at the Episcopal church had come under scrutiny after the man had been murdered by a local hate group.

Vaughn kept his arm around me and looked at Jack. "I haven't decided if I'm going to hug you or punch you yet."

"That's probably fair," Jack said. "I'll just stay over here until you figure it out."

"I'm surprised to see the two of you here," Vaughn said, looking at me. "Word on the street is that you moved into the funeral home."

"That part is true," Jack said. "At least for now."

Vaughn stroked my hair and then released me, moving to stand in front of the fireplace. He'd picked the drawing room of the old house for his office. There was all the modern convenience of a large desk and integrated technology, but the rest of the room looked as pristine and exact as it had probably been in the early 1900s.

The fire was making my eyes tired, so I moved to the Queen Anne sofa and curled up in the corner.

"Does that mean I'm not the only one who feels left out in knowing that you've got a kid?" Vaughn asked.

I could see the hurt in his eyes that Jack hadn't trusted him enough to tell him.

"No, I knew," I told him before things could escalate. "That's not the issue."

Vaughn looked at me thoughtfully and said, "There are so many issues I don't even know where to start. And I'm guessing since the tension in the room just skyrocketed a thousand percent that y'all haven't exactly worked things out, so I'll back off on that front. All I'm saying is a phone call or text would've been nice instead of finding out information the same way as everyone else."

Jack's lips quirked in a half smile. "I'll try to remember that for the next time."

"Very funny," Vaughn said. "You'll be glad to know you've raised more money in the past few days than in the last month. Floyd pissed a lot of people off when he printed that story. Everyone thinks he's playing too dirty, and that was a hit way below the belt. Your family has been here for generations."

"According to my mother," Jack said, "you'd think we were being taken over by outsiders and the founders are slowly fading away. It seems like everyone close to me has suffered because of Floyd. My mother was asked to resign her position as the fundraising chair at the country club. She yelled at me this morning about the article and then she burst into tears. Apparently, some woman complained because she thinks my behavior is scandalous. She also thinks that I'm holding King George back from progression. There are a lot of people who want those prisons here."

"No one with half a brain," Vaughn said, scoffing. "No one who wants to raise their children here or have a decent quality of life. This place is still mostly pure bloods. There are people in this county who are descendants of the founding fathers. The people pouring money into a moron like Floyd Parker are outsiders, and they're trying to sow discord and distract you from the endgame. And it's working. Look at the two of you. You're not even living in the same house. Your mother can't focus on campaign duties because she's been asked to step down from a position she's always taken pride in, and everyone who is close to you has been offered something sweet to switch loyalties so the contract for those prisons can be awarded. You need to get your head out of your ass and focus."

"They offered you money?" I asked Vaughn, sitting up straighter.

"They offered me 10 percent of a billion-dollar contract," he said, smiling. "I already have money, but that's *a lot* of money. You have to assume if they've approached me, then they've approached a lot of people who might be more than happy to take a fraction of that amount."

I swallowed, an uneasy feeling sweeping over me. Could we trust no one?

"I can't control what people do," Jack said. I heard the anger in his voice and was surprised by it. Jack rarely got angry. And when he was angry, he rarely showed it. "Politics is dirty. It's always been dirty. And it's driven by money. And money leads to power. There are few people in this country who can't be bought or who will do the right thing out of principle. I can feel them breathing down my neck every day, waiting to move in like a disease."

Jack's fist clenched and he got back to his feet. "Knowing that doesn't make me want to serve and protect. It makes me want to gather my family and escape to a place where no one will ever find us. You think I haven't had better job offers? Been asked to run for higher political offices? Of course I have. But I'm here, because here is what matters."

"It's going to be okay, Jack," Vaughn said. "The people here do appreciate you, even if they don't always show it. And I think, despite a few bad seeds sprinkled throughout, you might be surprised how many tell Floyd and those fancy investors to shove it."

"Can we do damage control at this point?" I asked. "The election is in four days."

"I actually think we're in good shape," Vaughn said. "And if what I've heard through the grapevine is true, then it's even better. Please tell me Floyd Parker really did turn himself in for a hit-and-run."

"He's up to something," I told Vaughn. "He didn't do it out of the goodness of his heart."

"I'll see if I can find out anything," he said. "I'm going to talk to your mother and my mother and we're going to rally. If anyone can get blood flowing again it's them."

"As nice as this is," Jack said, "we actually didn't come for a campaign meeting or couple's therapy."

"Well, you sure as hell need some," Vaughn said. "Consider this an added bonus. Why'd you come?"

"You haven't heard the identity of the victim from the hit-and-run this morning?" Jack asked. "The grapevine must be slipping."

"We've got a lot going on," he said. "And no. All talk of that stopped the second Floyd turned himself in. I heard he hit a guy on his bike out on 36. That's a bad stretch of road for biking. I've ridden it several times."

"If it's a bad stretch then why do you ride it?" I asked.

"Because it's the bad stretches that can be the most fun," he said, showing his teeth when he smiled. "That's what real cyclists crave." And then it was like the lightbulb finally switched on. "A real cyclist. It was someone from our club?"

"Brett Jorgenson," Jack said.

"Oh, man," Vaughn said, dropping down onto the other end of the sofa. "His wife is about to have a baby."

"We just came from there," I said.

Vaughn shook his head. "I don't know how you both do what you do. Doesn't it get depressing giving that kind of news to people all the time?"

"Yeah," Jack said. "It really does."

"So what do you need from me?" Vaughn asked. "Because of my amazing powers of deductive reasoning, I'm going to assume that maybe Floyd didn't have anything to do with Brett's death, and you're still trying to figure out who really killed him."

"With skills like that, you should be a cop," Jack said.

"God, no," Vaughn said. "And be a glutton for punishment? I'll leave that to you."

"Brett was murdered," I said, finally making the declaration out loud. "But it wasn't because of Floyd. I found lethal doses of amphetamines in his system. He had a massive heart attack as a result. I've never seen any heart damaged like his was."

Vaughn nodded. "Those hills would do it," he said. "I'm guessing you want to know if there's anyone in the group with a drug problem."

"That would be a good start," Jack said.

"I don't know of anyone," Vaughn said, "But it's mostly a social club. I don't really know anyone well enough to have that kind of information. There's certainly plenty of people in there who could afford a drug habit. It's an expensive sport."

"When was the last time you saw Brett?" Jack asked.

"At the ride last night," Vaughn said. "We ride three nights a week plus Saturday mornings. One Saturday a month we'll do a hundred-mile ride. Brett didn't ride with us on Mondays because he's in New York, but he always did the rest of the rides. And I know he rode every morning too."

"You ride a hundred miles on a bicycle?" I asked, thinking of what the glutes must feel like after that long in the saddle, and squeezing my legs together subconsciously.

"You get used to it," Vaughn said. "A few of the guys and I meet up with clubs all over the world in Italy every year and we ride a hundred miles a day until we get to Switzerland. Of course, when you have views like that it's a little different than riding through King George. I've tried to get you to come."

"Yes, I'm sure the taxpaying citizens want me to take a month off every year to ride my bike through the Alps," Jack said dryly. "Of course, come Tuesday I might have plenty of time to take it up again."

"Get real," Vaughn said, rolling his eyes. "There's no way in hell you'll lose this election. You've got to change your attitude. People here like to talk, but they're not stupid. Floyd has burned too many bridges over the years."

"He's also got a lot of friends who don't exactly care about doing things on the up-and-up," Jack said. "We just finished investigating John Donnelly's murder, and we discovered a whole network of people Floyd has in his pocket."

"So what?" Vaughn said. "Donnelly is dead, so that's a vote you don't have to worry about."

I laughed out loud and shook my head. "That's so wrong."

Vaughn smiled unrepentantly. "Just telling the truth."

"If we could stay on topic," Jack said. "Can you give us a list of everyone on the ride last night?"

"Sure," Vaughn said. "We only have about twenty riders that are dedicated enough to make all the group rides. Sometimes we'll do an open call for surrounding counties to join us if they want. Everything is done from our social media page. But last night we only had fifteen. Our numbers drop some this time of year when the weather is iffy and it gets dark so early.

"We have a different meeting place for each day we ride. On Saturdays we meet here at the store, since it's a longer route. We meet at six in the morning and then mostly stick to the perimeter of the county, or at least where there's nice paved roads. Monday nights we meet at six thirty at Mike Dunne's furniture store over in Newcastle. You remember him, Jack?"

Jack nodded. "Vaguely."

"On Wednesday night we meet at the Methodist Church in Nottingham and on Thursday nights we meet at Brett's house. Same time each night of the week."

"Wait, you meet at Brett's house?" Jack asked. "That's where you met last night?"

"Yeah," Vaughn said. "We only had fifteen show up last night. We picked Brett's house because it's exactly twenty miles to the square and twenty miles back. I arrived about six fifteen and we hit the road at six thirty. We made it back just before nine."

"It seems like you'd have to have a lot of organization for these rides," I said. "Routes, roads, traffic, time of day…"

"It takes some work," Vaughn agreed. "But we have a pretty consistent schedule now. Old Dominion is a club for more experienced riders, so we don't really have to deal with the newbies. We ride with lights on our bikes and helmets for night rides, but we stay in a group and keep pace."

"The hardest thing to figure out is going to be how he got the amphetamines in his system," I said. "If we can figure out the how I think we can get the who."

"The easiest way would be to drop them in his water bottles," Vaughn said.

"But how would that happen if he filled the water bottles up before he left for his ride?" I asked. "Unless someone put it in before he added the water. But the number of people who'd have access to his bottles is minimal."

Vaughn was smart and quick. "You're looking at Marla," he said. "But I can tell you there's no way she would or could do something like this. She's as sweet as they come. And she's been through it. Brett shared some of their history when we went out a couple of times for dinner. But there's really any number of people who'd have access."

"How?" I asked.

"Every rider on the team has habits and superstitions," Vaughn said. "I prep my gear and bike the same way each time. I like to think it brings me good luck. But when I do it the same way each time it also makes sure I've got everything I need when I'm out in the middle of nowhere. Brett was always ready to ride. He rode every morning like clockwork and then he did the three club rides per week, so I've watched how he preps. He immediately gets his bike and gear set up for the next ride as soon as he gets in from the ride he's on."

Jack nodded, understanding exactly where Vaughn was coming from.

"What?" I asked. "What am I missing?"

"When Brett got in from the ride last night, the first thing he did was put his bike on the wall in his garage, put his shoes on the rack, and refill his water bottles and put them back in the holders on the bike. He's got all his supplies there in the garage. If I want to get some extra miles in, I'll leave from here on my bike and ride out to his place on Thursdays before the official ride starts."

"You're all crazy," I said, shaking my head.

"It's an addiction," Vaughn said grinning. "It's the closest thing to flying without actually being in the air."

"That's what Marla said," I told him. "One addiction replaces another."

Vaughn nodded. "I agree. But what I was getting at was that when I'd get to his house on the bike he'd let me replenish there. He's got a filter on the sink out there, so I'd fill up my bottles, and he's got a cabinet full of GU gels and electrolyte tabs. But I'm telling you every time I've ever ridden with Brett his habits are the same. He always preps his bike, replenishes his zipper pouches, and refills his bottles immediately for the next ride."

"So anyone could have dropped the amphetamines in his bottles before they left for the night," Jack said.

Vaughn nodded. "I'll make you a list of everyone who rode last night."

"Were you the last to leave?" Jack asked.

"There were a few people who hung back after I took off," he said. "Last night was one of the nights I biked in, so I caught a ride back here to the store with Adam Taylor. I loaded my bike on his Jeep and we left a few minutes before nine."

"Would there have been a moment when someone could've slipped the drugs in the bottles?" I asked.

"Sure," Vaughn said, shrugging. "Anytime I guess. Some people bring an extra change of clothes and some use the bathroom. Their son is usually asleep by then, so everyone just uses the upstairs bathroom and office to change clothes. Sometimes we'll stand in the driveway just talking for twenty minutes. I don't think anyone ever really pays attention what anyone else is doing."

"I guess someone was counting on that," Jack said. "Let's see if we can smoke them out. Have room for an extra rider in the morning?"

9

"WE NEED TO SET UP A BOARD," JACK SAID AFTER
we'd left Vaughn. "We've got enough players to
start digging deeper, and it'll help to see it all
mapped out with timelines. We can set up the board
at the office if you're more comfortable there." He
paused for a moment and the tension between us had
my pulse racing. "Or we can go home."

My stomach flipped and I searched for the anger that
had been prevalent most of the day. But as much as I
tried to rekindle it, I'd found that most of my anger
had faded after we'd talked to Marla Jorgenson. The
hurt was still inside me, and there was a chasm
where there once hadn't been, but when it came
down to it, I believed in Jack. And I believed we
were stronger together than we were apart. And I
hoped that in the future, if I screwed up as badly as
he did, that he'd love me anyway and be able to
forgive me.

"Home is fine," I said, still unsure what that meant or what "home" was going to look like for the foreseeable future. But we had to start somewhere.

Jack was silent, and I watched out of my periphery as his knuckles tightened on the wheel.

"It's too late to do much more tonight," Jack said.

"I need to analyze those water bottles and make sure that's how the amphetamines were ingested. And we might be able to pull some prints from the outside of the bottle."

"Maybe," he said. "All the evidence is in lockup at the station. Tomorrow morning will be soon enough. Joining the ride will be a good way to observe how the team interacts. Maybe not everyone thought Brett Jorgenson was such a great guy. There's always a support van. You can catch a ride and follow us. Or you can join the ride."

"I think I'll pass," I said dryly. "I'm not sure my cycling skills can truly be appreciated by amateurs."

Jack choked on a laugh and ran a hand over the top of his head. He did that whenever his mind was elsewhere, even if it seemed like he was present in the conversation.

"You want to drive through and grab some dinner?" he asked.

I wasn't really hungry, but I nodded and Jack swung through and got a bucket of chicken and sides to go with it. It was a very un-Jack-like choice. His body was generally a temple. I frowned and looked at his profile.

"Everything okay?" I asked.

"Yeah, why?" he asked distractedly.

"'Cause this is about ten thousand calories," I said. "Not that I'm complaining, but you normally don't like your arteries filled with peanut oil and secret herbs and spices."

"I haven't eaten all day, and I figure I've already worked off that many calories running all over town today. I don't think a piece of chicken is going to set me on the path to dad-bod status."

"That's what everyone with a dad bod says," I told him. "And then before you know it you're only wearing sweatpants for all four seasons."

"I'm glad you found your sense of humor," he said sardonically. "Really, it's like a breath of fresh air."

I felt the grin split my face before I could help it and a laugh bubbled out. And then I started to cry and couldn't seem to stop—great, gulping sobs that had me hunched over and wrapping my arms around my middle.

Jack pulled the car to the side of the road. I don't know how he did it, but he had my seat belt unbuckled and he maneuvered himself across the console, lifting me and sliding into the seat, cradling me in his arms. He let me cry, but I was very aware that his body trembled as well and that his tears dampened the side of my neck.

"I'm so sorry," he said.

All I could do was nod against his chest and squeeze his hand. A few minutes later I said, "I was so angry with you."

"I know, I know," he whispered, rocking me back and forth. "You have every right to be."

"It's pointless," I said, sitting up straight and wiping the tears from my cheeks. I saw the stricken look on Jack's face, and I realized he thought I meant *we* were pointless.

"Jaye," he said, shaking his head.

"No, no," I corrected. "I mean it's pointless to be angry. We're not doing each other any good right now with this between us. Vaughn was right. Floyd got what he wanted when he separated us. I forgive you. But don't you ever do that to me again. You can't doubt me. You're the only constant I've ever had in my life. No one has ever believed in me but you. Don't take that away from me. We're it. We're all we've got. That's what family is. If you can't trust anyone else, you have to trust me. And I have to be able to trust you."

I stared into the dark fathoms of his eyes and saw the pain there, and I would've given anything to be able to take it from him.

"My life," Jack said, leaning his head back against the seat and closing his eyes. "The things I've done in this life. The people I've hurt. The things I've seen. It plants seeds of doubt—in others and in myself. It's the nature of the job. There's always a part of me that holds something back. Just in case. Even with you. I'm just…afraid."

That was the last thing I expected for him to say, and all I could do was stare at him for a few seconds. "Afraid of what?" I finally asked.

"We've been given a gift," he said. "I should be dead. Hell, maybe we should both be dead after everything we've gone through. But we're here. I've lived a blessed life. I've had a career I love, and I have you, who for some reason loves me back.

"And sometimes I wonder if God will one day realize that He's given me too many chances. Sometimes I wonder if everything we have now will just all go away. And the thought of losing you scares the living daylights out of me. Because the man I am now is because of you. It's you who makes the nightmares go away. It's you who makes me think of a future. It's you who makes me want to be and do better."

I thought I might be out of tears, but I felt more sliding down my cheeks.

"I know that I grew up entitled and fast and easy," he said. "I never gave much thought to personal relationships. I always had you guys. We ran in a tight circle. But women never meant much to me. They came and went, and it didn't really matter who filled the spot in my bed. I figured I'd eventually meet someone who was worth settling down for and I'd have a marriage like my parents do. And then I met Lydia. She was older and sophisticated and she was on the prowl for anyone who could give her that forbidden excitement. I thought I was an adult, but I was in no way mature enough to handle someone like her.

"When she told me she was pregnant, that was the first time I saw…" He paused to think. "I don't know if remorse is the right word. But she was definitely aware that there were consequences to actions. I have no idea what her marriage was like. We never talked about anything personal. But her husband was someone important. And there was a thread of fear in her—of panic—at the idea of leaving him or telling him the truth.

"I thought I was doing the right thing—the noble thing—by telling her I'd take her away and we could raise the baby together. She was almost as horrified by that as she was by her husband. I didn't love her, but I'd talked myself into believing I could love her. So when I realized she had no feelings for me whatsoever, so much that she'd never even consider letting me be a father or trying to be a man or a husband, it shifted something in me."

He stroked my hair as he spoke, but I could tell he was a million miles away. "It was like being punched in the face and then being held under water until I almost drowned. I won't lie and say that didn't do some damage, because it did.

"It changed something in me—in the way I saw myself and my future. I never believed I was entitled to a happily-ever-after. I stopped thinking about wanting the kind of marriage my parents had, and I went on with my life. I joined the military. I embraced bachelorhood. But you were always there, doing your own thing, having your own life. You moved away, and still I thought about you. I thought at first because we had the kind of friendship that had bonded us for a couple of decades. But then I realized it was something much more—much deeper than that.

"I knew the moment you moved back home that I'd only put myself on the bench. I hadn't taken myself completely out of the game. And it helped that I knew you so well, because I was able to bide my time and slip under your guard little by little. I knew you were grieving and hurting over your parents.

And I knew that day in my office when you came to confront me, that something had switched in that brain of yours and you realized I could be more than just a friend."

He smiled then, and it was easy to recall the memory of that day, of questioning feelings I never thought possible for Jack.

"I'd never wanted to kiss someone and strangle them at the same time before," he said. "But I knew that was it for me. I knew that you were it, and I'd do whatever it took to plant you by my side for eternity."

I searched for something to dry my face and finally gave up and used my scarf.

"But it still doesn't erase the fact that I made a child and he's out there somewhere, and I'm a complete stranger to him. I could've fought Lydia and made things difficult, but the only person who would've really suffered is a child. But it's come back to bite me anyway. Now everyone around me is suffering. You, my parents, my friends. All for what? A secret I was too ashamed to share."

"That's where shame thrives," I told him. "When you keep those secrets in the dark. Can you imagine the rally of support you'd have had if everyone hadn't been blindsided by that news? Floyd would've had no power over you. But Floyd prospers in those hidden places. But the dark doesn't stand a chance against the light."

I touched the side of his face, and then I leaned my forehead against his. I'd missed the comfort of his touch. "You're a good man, Jack. And whatever you've done in your past, you don't deserve to suffer. This is not punishment. We all make mistakes. We're human. And that's what humans do. Even you. But the more you live in the past—regret the past—and hold on to that shame from the past, the harder it's going to be to move into the future you were called to have."

"Wow," he said, kissing me softly. "Wise words."

"I know," I said. "Let's go home. I'm starving."

10

I'D LIVED ON HERESY ROAD MY ENTIRE LIFE.

It backed up to the Potomac and was about as far away as you could get from civilization in the county. The house I'd lived in with my parents had been at one end of the two-mile stretch of road, and my time there hadn't been filled with happy memories. I'd been all for demolishing it to the ground, but Jack had a more practical nature and had renovated and sold it to another couple.

The house Jack had built several years ago was at the other end of the two-mile stretch. It had seemed odd for a single man to live so far out in the country, but Jack had always valued his privacy. His parents had always been very involved in the community—his father holding various political offices and his mother chairing social committees—so he'd always felt like he lived in somewhat of a fishbowl.

I wasn't sure what I was expecting after being away the last couple of days. I didn't know if it would still feel like home. Jack obviously still had insecurities about the life he deserved, but he wasn't the only one. Sometimes my marriage to Jack felt surreal, as if I didn't quite deserve the husband and home I'd always longed for.

But it was relief I felt when the house came into view. The lights were on, and it was like a beacon amidst the trees as we turned into the drive. I'd always loved this house, even before it was mine, and I'd always envied Jack that he'd had the vision to see what it could be, even before a single board was nailed into place.

It was three stories of logs and glass—a modern-day log cabin—that looked like it had been carved from the trees that surrounded it and the cliff it perched on. From our third-floor bedroom windows we could see the tops of the towering pines—as if we were sleeping in a tree house—and we could hear the rushing water of the Potomac at the base of the cliff.

I'd left my Suburban at the funeral home, which meant if I was going to get those bottles tested in the lab tomorrow then I'd have to get up early and go with Jack to talk with the cyclists. I'd had dreams of sleeping in my own bed and getting a solid twelve hours of sleep, and I was excited for the dreams to become reality.

I was mentally and physically exhausted after my tears had run their course and the weight of our conversation, and I stood in our foyer and breathed in my surroundings. It felt good to be home.

"We should get a dog," I said out of the blue. I was thinking it would be nice to have someone to greet us when we came home.

Jack looked at me strangely for a second and then said, "I was just thinking the exact same thing. Harley Gross's bitch just had a litter of puppies. They're farm dogs, but we probably could use a dog with some size way out here."

I took off my coat and hung it in the closet and tossed my scarf on the entry table so I could put it in the wash later. And then I headed straight to Jack's office. I wasn't interested in sitting down at the table. Despite my exhaustion, I had a strange energy about me that wanted to get things done. I wanted to find who killed Brett Jorgenson. And then I wanted to hunt down and destroy Floyd Parker however we could.

It was time Floyd stopped coming after me and those I loved. He was an enemy. And I was done letting him dictate the terms of our future.

"Eat first," Jack said. "Destroy later." I gave him a confused look. "You have a look on your face that makes me a little worried for Floyd and very worried as a police officer."

I smiled, showing a lot of teeth, and Jack raised his brows. "There have to be some perks to being married to the sheriff."

Most of the bottom floor of the house was brand new thanks to my parents. A few months back they'd decided to turn our living room into the O.K. Corral. Clearly marriage counseling hadn't worked for them.

As aggravating as it was to have people in the house wielding hammers and other things that made loud noises, I'd enjoyed the process of rebuilding more than I thought I would. It had given me the opportunity to make the home ours instead of just Jack's. And it was nice to see my touches and ideas scattered here and there.

But Jack's office was all his, and the renovation there had taken the longest because of the upgraded technology that had been incorporated into the room. Which ironically, would mostly go unused if Jack lost the election, but it had been an interesting experiment to see the kinds of things that were available if you had the money to pay for it. It also helped to have friends in high places who knew exactly how far was too far before federal law kicked in.

The thought of having all that advanced technology really put the upcoming election into perspective. I'd run through the scenarios in my mind of what it might be like if I resigned my position, but I hadn't really thought about what it might be like if Jack lost. It was best not to let my mind even go there. I couldn't imagine the damage and corruption that would become King George if Floyd won.

We probably spent more time in Jack's office than we did the rest of the house. It was comfortable. Even in our downtime we often watched movies snuggled on the deep leather sofa with a fire crackling beside us.

The whole office was decorated in shades of blue and green, from the art on the walls to the plush throws over the furniture to the rugs on the floor. Jack's desk was big and L-shaped and had been handmade by a local woodworker, and there was a conference table to the side of the room made of an old barn door. The whole west side wall was windows, but the blackout shades had lowered when the sun set. The fireplace was made of stone, and the ceiling was pine planks.

But my favorite addition to the room was the whiteboard wall that covered the area behind and adjacent to Jack's desk. It was completely electronic and could be used as a giant touchscreen computer. It was fast and efficient when it came to setting up murder boards.

I saw Jack put the chicken on the conference table out of my periphery, and then he went to the fireplace to start a fire. I took a seat behind his desk and logged into the desktop under my account.

Thanks to Jack, everything at the sheriff's office was now digital, so I was able to pull up the autopsy and crime scene photos. I also pulled up Brett's DMV photo and placed it in the center of the board.

Sometimes the cases we worked could become methodical, so it helped to keep the faces of those affected front and center, and then from there we built a spiderweb of a network that would link anyone who interacted with the victim, could benefit from his death, or who might have a grudge or bad business dealing with the victim. It could get very entangled and messy before things started to sort themselves out.

"Want me to make you a plate?" Jack asked.

"Sure," I said. "Dark meat. Extra coleslaw."

"I guess that counts as a vegetable," Jack said.

I grunted and brought Marla Jorgenson's picture on-screen, placing it next to her husband's on the board.

"She'd have access anytime she wanted to those water bottles, and she knew his schedule better than anyone," I said. "It still could have been her. Maybe she did it last night for the specific reason that so many people were at the house and suspicion could be thrown on anyone."

"But why?" Jack said, making his own plate and sitting on the edge of the desk. "They've lived in King George for three years. Why would she pick this moment in time to kill him after all the years they've been together? What's significant about the timing?"

"It's Friday," I said. "He'd leave for work again on Sunday night. She said he works in finance on Wall Street. And money is always a motive for murder. Though I guess depending on how Marla comes out with life insurance and assets, money could be her motive there too."

I took a bite of chicken and closed my eyes at the pure pleasure that coursed through me. I was ravenous, and I had to remind myself to eat slow so I didn't swallow everything whole. I should have known better, both as a doctor and as an adult, but my eating habits had always been somewhat juvenile, and Jack had just learned not to say anything. Though I could usually hear his mental scolding.

I stopped eating when Vaughn's picture popped up on the whiteboard, another link to the forming web.

"Really?" I asked.

"There were fifteen people at the Jorgenson house last night, including his wife," Jack said. "Vaughn was one of them. I can't leave him out just because he's our friend, even though I don't believe he had anything to do with it. He's got money, connections, and he more than likely knows someone who could sell him amphetamines. And if whoever slipped the drugs into Jorgenson's water bottles was in the bike club, then Vaughn knows the killer personally."

"They're all going to have a connection in some capacity," I said. "We're looking for money and access and ties outside of the cycling club."

"We also need to consider something that might be a very possible reality," Jack said. "We might have a finite amount of time to solve this case. It could take months to get a warrant for beneficiary and life insurance information. And if we start digging into Wall Street it might be months longer or never. They don't really like to let go of that kind of information easily."

I considered what he was saying. "First of all, you're going to win. We've got to change our mindset and think positive. Second of all, you could call a friend and see if he could speed up the process."

Jack blew out a breath. "Yeah, I could call a friend. But I feel like the favors are going to start running out soon. Saving a person's life will only get you so far."

"I don't think Carver feels that way," I said. "Michelle might if he keeps getting her pregnant. But Carver would lie down in the middle of the street for you."

"Maybe one day someone will tell Carver how babies are made," Jack said. He opened his laptop and the screen was shared on the whiteboard. "Do you have the list of names Vaughn gave you?" he asked.

"Right here," I said, unfolding the heavy stationery with Vaughn's neat block lettering on it.

"Start running backgrounds and getting them on the board," he said. "I'll deal with Carver."

I typed in the first name on the list. Leslie Carron. And I let the computer run while Carver's face popped up on the wall.

"What in the hell is going on in Bloody Mary?" Carver said by way of greeting. "I just left a few days ago and everything was fine. And now I'm getting news all the way in DC about the two of you? I'm in a wheelchair, but I will come down there and knock both your heads together."

"Wow," Jack said. "Sounds like you're feeling better. They must have amped up your physical therapy for all that attitude."

Carver's face broke into a smile. It was nice to see, especially considering he had months of physical therapy and surgeries in front of him.

"You like that?" Carver asked. "I've been practicing my bad cop routine for when I can get back out in the field."

"You should probably practice your shooting instead," Jack teased. "I still don't know how you got field certified. Someone must owe you a lot of favors."

"Well, I'm kind of in charge of a lot of people and a lot of things," Carver said. "I can pretty much do what I want."

"That explains it," Jack said.

"But seriously," Carver said. "Are you guys okay? I know it's been less than a week since I've seen you, but somehow you've gained a son and lost a wife in that time. Maybe Michelle and I should move closer to keep an eye on you." Carver looked back over his shoulder to make sure his wife wasn't listening. "Where's J.J.?"

"I'm right here," I told him, moving into the camera view.

"I'm not a doctor," Carver said. "But you look like you could use some sleep."

"I'm kind of getting tired of people telling me that," I said. "People have no manners anymore."

Carver grinned unrepentantly. "I blame it on social media. I've always thought you were too pretty. I think it's nice to see you looking like the rest of us."

I laughed and decided It felt good. Maybe a dose of Carver was just what I needed. "I'm doing okay," I assured him. "We're doing okay. Election season is brutal."

"Tell me about it," he said. "I could be fired at any time based on who's sitting in the White House. I try not to let it get me down. And I might have told the president that if he fired me I'd hack into all of his accounts and rob him blind. He knows I was kidding. Kind of."

"We don't mean to interrupt your Friday night," Jack said.

"Are you kidding me?" Carver asked. "Michelle's book club is meeting downstairs and my mother-in-law is watching the girls. My Friday night consists of avoiding estrogen at all costs. Tell me you have something for me to do. I could organize your files or siphon money from your opponent's campaign account into yours. You tell me how I can be most useful."

Jack laughed. "Thank God you're on the side of the good guys."

"Meh," Carver said. "I like to leave my options open. And technically I'm still on medical leave, so I'm not representing the FBI right at this moment. I don't know. It's kind of a gray area. But I have had the chance to try to hack all of the government data-bases. You'll be glad to know ours is secure. But the Pentagon needs some work. I sent them a memo. We should probably talk fast because you never know when a platoon is going to show up at the door and carry me away."

"He makes me so tired," I said under my breath. "I don't know how Michelle does it."

"I'm sitting right here you know," Carver said. "I can hear you. But sometimes I wonder how Michelle does it too. There's been a time or two I suspected she put something in my drink at night to help me sleep. Maybe you could investigate that."

"I'm sure you'll be fine," Jack said. "But call me if your hair starts falling out in chunks or you have constant diarrhea."

"You're starting to sound like Michelle," he said, narrowing his eyes. "Tell me what you need before I hang up on you and go feel sorry for myself."

"We caught a case today," Jack said. "I'm a little worried about the timing because it's going to call for digging into financials that could take months to process. And I might not have months as sheriff."

Carver was never one to be serious for long. I often wondered about that—if his joviality was a mask for something deeper. But his mouth creased in a hard line and his brow furrowed in thought.

"First of all, I don't think that's going to happen," Carver said, and then he held up a finger before Jack could interrupt. "I'm not saying it can't happen, but I looked into the polls in your area and incumbents always run a strong race. Secondly, I've already taken the liberty of compiling a file against your opponent, just in case you feel it's necessary. He's getting a large amount from one particular donor. I haven't been able to get the identity of the donor yet, only the city and two front corporations I can't find an owner or board of directors for, which tells me whoever it is has a lot of money and a lot of political power."

"Why would someone from DC care what happens in the election here in King George?" I asked.

"That's the question," Carver said. "But I can think of some reasons."

"The federal prisons," Jack said, nodding.

"Bingo," Carver said. "There are a lot of people sitting on the opposite side of the aisle than you who could make millions by having those prisons built in King George. You're talking about a billion-dollar federal contract. There are lobbyists and contractors and politicians and investors who would happily slit your throat and dance on your grave to see those prisons become a reality."

I looked at Jack's face, but he didn't seem surprised by this information. "You knew it was this bad?" I asked. "Why didn't you tell me?"

"What is there to do about it?" Jack asked. "I'm here to serve the people of King George and their best interests. I don't care what donors or people outside this county want. They don't live here. And the people in this county don't want their farms plowed under so those prisons can be built. They don't want the worst dregs of society being sent across the Potomac and housed down the road from them. And they really don't want to pay a tax increase so they can help lower their quality of life. So whoever is donating to Floyd's campaign can keep wasting money. I'm not changing my mind."

"Which leads me to my third point," Carver said. "If you do happen to lose, you can finally come work for the FBI."

"I'd make a terrible FBI agent," Jack said. "There are too many rules and regulations. And I've found I like being the boss. Maybe I'll just run for governor instead. Or maybe we'll live off our investments and become recluses and raise chickens."

I pressed my lips together at that. "Maybe we could start with the dog," I said. "I'm not sure I'm meant to have chickens that don't come from a supermarket."

"Amen, sister," Carver said. "I knew I liked you."

I watched Jack's body relax. Carver was Jack's best friend, but I'd come to the realization throughout the day that we both had really good friends. Even when we weren't good to each other.

"So what have you got for me?" Carver asked.

"We caught a homicide this morning," Jack said.

"You don't sound 100 percent sure on that," Carver said.

"We got a call in for a cyclist on the side of the highway," I said. "It looked like a standard hit-and-run. The bike was pretty mangled. But when I got him back to the lab I found high traces of amphetamines in his system. Official cause of death was cardiac arrest."

"Yeah, that'll do it," Carver said. "Those things are hell on the heart. Never could understand why athletes would take the chance."

"That's the thing," Jack said. "He's not a pro. He belongs to one of the local cycling clubs. But the victim is some kind of Wall Street analyst. We're talking big money."

"So since you're calling me, I'm assuming you don't think the doping was his choice."

"I called it a homicide, and I think we're on the right track," I said. "But the victim has a drug history, which makes it tricky. Cocaine for the most part, and it did damage to the heart and lungs. Any defense attorney would take that and have a field day."

"All you can do is collect the evidence," Carver said. "The attorneys will feed on themselves and take everyone's money. You can't worry about them."

"This guy was brilliant," Jack said, "but apparently he liked the adrenaline rush."

"You don't get into the Wall Street rat race unless you do," Carver said. "Drugs are prevalent on Wall Street, so I'm not surprised. When you make that kind of money it's easy to run out of things to spend it on.

"Then their behavior gets more depraved and goes way past the point of legal. Then you end up with Jeffrey Epstein types. Wall Street is a mess. It's politics and corruption and everything in between." But there was a gleam in Carver's bright blue eyes. "And there's nothing I like more than digging into corruption. Of course, anything I find in the periphery is inadmissible, but it should be enough to get you started on your murder so you can find a thread to tug. Give me a name and we'll start with the basics."

While Jack sent Carver Marla's information, I studied the data on Leslie Carron and then started the next search while I read her file.

She was a forty-year-old divorcee who worked as an engineer for a petroleum plant in Richmond, but she lived in Newcastle like a lot of the people who worked in Richmond. I put her picture up next to Vaughn's and studied her face. She was pretty, in an understated way, and she didn't have a criminal history, or even a parking ticket for that matter.

Adam Taylor was the next person on the list, and I looked at him closely, remembering that Vaughn had mentioned the name. They'd ridden home together the night before. There'd been something in

Vaughn's voice when he'd mentioned the name that made me feel very protective.

Adam Taylor's picture went up on the whiteboard, the spiderweb extending out from Vaughn's picture.

I added the time Adam and Vaughn left the Jorgenson house to the timeline and watched it organize itself on the far right of the wall.

My first thought when I saw Taylor's picture was *military*, and then I didn't have to scroll down too far to see that I was right. He'd been stationed at the naval base in King George for the last three years. Caucasian male. Six foot one. A hundred and seventy-five pounds. His jaw was angular and he was clean shaven, and his driver's license said his hair was brown, even though in his picture it was cropped too close to tell for sure. He was twenty-nine, never been married, and he'd been deployed once. He was currently ranked as a first lieutenant.

I made my way down the list and saw it was pretty evenly matched as far as men and women went. There were two married couples. I went ahead and put them on the board, but I separated them, thinking it was more unlikely for it to be a duo in on a hit.

Harry and Connie Morgan were in their early sixties. She was a retired schoolteacher and he'd retired from banking earlier in the year. I did put an asterisk next to his name because of the finance connection, but it seemed like a long shot. It looked like Harry and Connie had spent their year cycling and going on cruises. They seemed to be enjoying retired life immensely.

Next were Mitch and Gloria Padgett. Both of them dentists in their early fifties. They had several dentist offices throughout the county, and it looked like they did very well for themselves. Two daughters in college. A nice house in an established neighborhood that was completely paid for, and it looked like they bought a new car every three years, always a BMW.

Every time I got information I sent it on to Carver so he could do the next level of digging. But so far there was no one who stood out as being a potential murderer, though Benji Lyles did have an arrest on his record for possession of cocaine. But it was a twenty-year-old charge and no time had been served. He'd gotten off with community service.

Jack gave a long, low whistle and my head jerked up to see what he was looking at. There were numbers scrolling across the screen at a rapid pace, and I had no idea what they meant.

"What's that?" I asked.

"The Jorgensons' many numerous accounts," Jack said. "They've got stock holdings, bank accounts, retirement accounts, bonds, real estate, and every other type of investment you could possibly think of. They have no debt, and their son and the new baby both have college funds and trust accounts.

Brett and Marla are both signers on all accounts. Any account solely in one name has the other listed as beneficiary. Brett was very smart with their money, and at this point their money is just making more money."

"Anything illegal?" I asked. "Life insurance?"

"No policies that I could find," Carver said. "Typically at this level of income life insurance policies aren't needed. It would look more suspicious if they did have a policy."

"Why's that?" I asked.

"Because policies are typically taken out to cover debt in case a spouse dies," he said. "If Marla had a policy on Brett or vice versa, I'd be looking hard to see if either had hidden accounts or had maybe made a bad investment somewhere. But there's nothing like that I can find."

"Okay," I said. "So we put Marla on the back burner. Which I'm glad because she seemed like a genuinely good person. That leaves the thirteen other people who met at the Jorgenson house."

"Did you find anyone who stands out as a killer?" Jack asked.

"Strangely enough," I said, "there could be several candidates."

"Sounds like a hell of a bike club," Carver said, raising his brows in surprise. "Did the Hells Angels change rides?"

"Nothing quite that exciting," I said, smiling at the mental picture that gave me. "But there were fourteen members on last night's ride, fifteen including the victim. Let's say for the sake of expediency that our friend Vaughn is in the clear, that leaves thirteen potential suspects. Of the remaining suspects, three are doctors and would have access to amphetamines. Four are in finance in some capacity or other. Two have military ties, and one has a cocaine charge."

"What about the last three?" Carver asked.

"A schoolteacher, an engineer, and an attorney," I said. "Probability seems low, though all are women and drugging someone tends to be a woman's method of murder. As far as who these people are, I'm not sure how they'd be connected to Brett Jorgenson. None of them share common workplaces with him and none of them are from New York."

"Maybe something will pop on the financial," Carver said. "This will give me something to do tonight when insomnia kicks in."

"You're still not sleeping at night?" Jack asked.

Carver shrugged. "It comes and goes," he said. "But it's always best to have something to occupy my mind."

Jack studied his friend closely, and I felt like a voyeur intruding on his private thoughts. Carver's face went unreadable as Jack stared at him, and I wondered what Carver was trying to hide from Jack.

"Y'all stay out of trouble," Carver said. "And watch your back. Someone has taken a big interest in your campaign. When there's money at stake there's always an element of danger involved."

"Are you talking about Jack or the case?" I asked.

"Both," Carver said. "Sleep tight." And then he disconnected and his face disappeared from the whiteboard.

"What was that all about?" I asked. "Why isn't Carver sleeping? And why's he trying to hide it from you?"

"Sometimes sleep is the worst thing you can do in our line of work," Jack said. "Because then the dreams come and you wake up in a cold sweat, trying to remember where you are and why you're still alive. It started after we left the Marines. But you don't talk about it. You just pretend it doesn't exist and you move on. We both finished college while in the military and we both moved on to law enforcement, though in very different aspects. But there are things in the world of war that can't ever be unseen or undone, it doesn't matter if it's on our own soil or someone else's. Some days it gets easier and you think it's gone away. And then some nights it comes back in full force and you watch the window and pray for the sun to come up."

"PTSD," I said.

Jack nodded. "Everyone finds their coping mechanism."

"What's yours?" I asked.

He shut down the computer and the wall screen went blank. "You are," he said, reaching for my hand and taking it in his. "We've got an early morning ahead of us. Let's go to bed."

I squeezed his hand and studied his face, but it was clear and there was peace. I didn't see any of the demons there that were tormenting Carver.

11

IT WAS THE FIRST SOLID NIGHT'S SLEEP I'D HAD IN A while, and morning had come much too soon.

I looked at the clock on the bedside table and corrected that thought. Morning wasn't the right word. It was still the middle of the night, and everyone should be asleep. I couldn't imagine what kind of insane person wanted to get up at this time to ride a bicycle in the dark around the county, but apparently they existed.

I heard the shower running, and I smelled coffee, but I snuggled under the blanket a little longer. I was naked and felt like a lazy, satisfied cat, and the last thing I wanted to do was go stand in the cold with a bunch of people in spandex. But such was life.

I lifted the covers enough to reach for the coffee mug, thankful that Jack was a creature of habit and loved mornings as much as I despised them, and I managed to position myself so I didn't spill hot coffee on my skin as I took my first sip.

I heard the water turn off and a few seconds later I saw the lights come on from beneath my cocoon and Jack snorted with laughter at the sight of me.

"I'm going to assume the giant lump is you under there," he said. "Better hit the shower if you want to talk to our suspects."

I slowly pulled the covers down from over my head and let my eyes adjust to the light.

"You're not terrible to look at first thing in the morning," I told him. He was standing in the doorway between the bed and the bathroom with only a towel wrapped low on his hips and droplets of water on his shoulders. The scars on his chest and ribs were a constant reminder of how lucky I was he was still here, and the tattoo on his hip was a reminder that he really liked for that spot to be kissed.

I blew a strand of hair out of my face and Jack grinned. I knew my morning appearance wasn't nearly as appealing as Jack's. "Maybe we should just call it a day and get back in bed."

"Sex is the downfall of athletes everywhere," he said, tossing his towel over the hook and heading to the dresser to pull out clothes. "You never have sex before a big race. You'll lose every time."

"I guess it's a good thing my racing days are over," I said, tossing back the covers and climbing out of bed. When the election was over Tuesday I vowed to spend the rest of the week in bed as much as possible. Election season was exhausting. Murder was exhausting. And relationships were exhausting. I'd hit the exhausting triumvirate.

I padded the way to the bathroom, thankful for heated floors, and I finished my coffee in the shower. It was Saturday, and the last remaining tornado victim was scheduled for a memorial later in the afternoon, and her funeral was tomorrow. I trusted Lily, Emmy Lu, and Sheldon (kind of), to finish off the weekend strong. And I was going to keep my fingers crossed we didn't get any new arrivals between now and election day. The whole staff was going to need a vacation before this was over.

I dressed casual and warm, thinking about the morning spent at the lab collecting samples from the water bottles and having them fingerprinted, and then I hurried down the stairs, knowing Jack was waiting for me.

"Hello, spandex," I said when I saw him in the kitchen, pouring a to-go mug of coffee for me. He was dressed a lot like Brett Jorgenson when we found his body, and the thought gave me pause. A cyclist would never be a match for a car. The roads were slick and visibility wasn't great.

"As hot as you look," I said, "I'm not sure this is the best idea for you to ride with the group. And don't forget one of them is a murderer."

"It's been a few years, but I know what I'm doing," he said. And then he grinned wickedly. "It'll be just like—"

"No, don't say it," I said, shaking my head.

"Riding a bike," he finished.

I blew out a sigh and took the to-go mug from him. "You're in a good mood this morning."

"What's not to be in a good mood about? I woke up this morning. That's always a plus considering the alternative. I woke up next to a beautiful, naked woman, who happens to be the love of my life and my wife. Also a plus. And I'm about to hit the open road and do something I love and haven't made the time for.

"There's only so many things in life we can control," he said. "All this other stuff that's happening around us? That's out of our control. Come Tuesday whatever happens, happens. That's the American way. I've poured everything into this job the last four years, but this election has made me realize that I can't pour into everyone and everything else and not pour into me. We tend to get wrapped in work, especially since we do it together, but I'm going to start taking my days off. I'm going to start doing the things I love again. And I'm going to make sure that we're taking the time together we need to stay a tight unit. Politics is dirty, and it can take a toll. I didn't realize how much until this last week."

"Does this mean I need to find a hobby?" I asked. "Don't get me wrong, I've always been grateful that you're into fitness and exercise and health because I clearly reap the benefits—last night exhibit A. My enjoyment comes from more sedentary entertainment."

"Till death do us part, right?" Jack said, leading me to the front to get our coats. He carried a black gym bag.

I was trying to figure out if the till death do us part comment was meant as a warning that my lack of health consciousness would lead to an early death, but I was enjoying the morning too much. It was nice to feel like I was back on solid ground.

Jack had left his Tahoe in the garage and chosen his pickup instead. It was sitting in the driveway with the ignition and headlights turned on. It was still dark outside. His bike was in a rack in the back, and I couldn't remember ever seeing it. Though to be fair, there was a lot of stuff in the garage that fell into the "toy" category that I wasn't familiar with. He tossed the black bag in the bed, and I hurried around to the passenger side and opened the door.

I wasn't a fan of getting weather this cold this early in the year. It didn't bode well for the months ahead.

At least the rain had cleared off for now, though I wasn't sure how long it was going to hold off.

"Are any of the club members holdovers from when you were involved?" I asked, snuggling into the seat and thankful for seat warmers and the fact that I had a husband who thought about things like warming the car before you got in. I never remembered that stuff.

"A couple of them," he said. "Mitch and Gloria Padgett are longtime riders. They're dentists. Ginny Grant was there when I was riding and so was Mario Ricci and Benji Lyles. And Vaughn of course. Everyone else is new to me though. There were only fourteen that showed up Thursday night for the ride, plus Brett, but there are probably a couple of hundred people in the bike club. You'll have stragglers that'll catch a ride or two a week, but it's few that are diehards and will catch every ride. The women tend to be divorced or young and single."

"Husband hunters?" I asked.

Jack's mouth quirked in a smile. "Something like that," he said. "There have been several hookups over the years, a couple that led to marriage. Like I said, it's a social club."

There was no traffic on the way to King George, but when we pulled into the parking lot at Vaughn's it was full of cars and bicycles. There were bikes everywhere, propped against the railing and vehicles. I'd never seen anything like it.

It was complete chaos as people walked around half dressed in the cold, steam rising from bodies and breath. There was an undercurrent of excitement, as groups huddled together and spoke in hushed whispers, as bikes were looked over and admired.

"This is a heck of a lot more than fourteen people," I said.

"They're wearing black armbands," Jack said, pointing out the black strip of cloth wrapped around everyone's biceps. "It looks like they're doing a memorial ride for Brett. Usually when there's a special ride they'll announce it on social media and other clubs from the state are welcome to join."

"Oh, good," I said. "That should make our job much easier."

"Look," Jack said, pointing to a group standing on the far side of the lot. "That's Old Dominion. They're wearing blue and silver. Each of the team clubs have their own colors."

"It really is like the Hells Angels of bicycles," I said.

"Don't tell Carver," Jack said. "He'll be disappointed he missed it. Though typically people in this tax bracket don't resort to barroom brawls and back-alley stabbings. But they do have their fair share of drama."

We parked and I watched in fascination as Jack got his bike from the rack and then went through the routine of putting various things in pouches and pockets. He wore an Old Dominion jersey like the others, and he pulled on a skullcap and arm warmers with practiced ease. He put on his cycling shoes, and then he was clip-clopping his way across the pavement like everyone else.

I followed close behind, content to be more of an observer. I recognized most everyone from their pictures. There were a couple of extras who hadn't been on the Thursday ride, so I wasn't as interested in them.

"Sheriff," Mitch Padgett said, coming over to shake Jack's hand. His teeth were perfect and blindingly white, which I guess was a good advertisement considering his profession. "Good to see you back on a ride. Terrible shame about Brett. He was a good guy. You've got mine and Gloria's support for the election. I think Vaughn would kick us out of the group if we didn't support you." His handshake was enthusiastic, and Jack skillfully extracted himself from the guy's grip.

I looked among the faces of the crowd and stopped when I came across Leslie Carroll. She'd been watching the exchange between Mitch and Jack, and she didn't seem too happy to hear that Mitch was throwing his support behind Jack if her scowl said anything about it.

Vaughn came up and slapped Jack on the back good-naturedly and tossed him an armband. "We decided to dedicate the ride to Brett," he said. "We should have close to a hundred riders today."

Jack's lips pressed together and he gave Vaughn a side-eye. "I don't suppose you let the sheriff's office know the route or anything like that to help with traffic?"

Vaughn winced. "It was kind of a last-minute thing. Besides, we're taking off in shifts so it's not so crowded on the roads. Each team leader has the route and their start time. It'll work out okay."

"Oh, Mrs. Lawson," Mitch said, stopping directly in front of me. No one ever called me Mrs. Lawson, so it took me a minute to figure out who he was talking to. "Are you riding in the support van? I'm glad to see you here. I was telling Gloria just the other day that you couldn't believe everything you saw in the media. We'll see y'all Tuesday night at the watch party. We're good friends with Jack's mom and dad."

I gave him a genuine smile and a thank-you, but I kept an eye on Leslie Carroll to see if she'd been listening. She was in conversation with Zoe Krantz, a young black woman I knew to be a local attorney from her background check, but I could tell Leslie was paying close attention to what was going on with Jack. Interesting.

"Hey, man," Adam Taylor said, coming up behind Vaughn and hitting him in the shoulder. "Adam Taylor." He stuck his hand out to Jack's for an introduction.

"Jack Lawson," Jack said. "Nice to meet you."

Adam Taylor was even better looking in person than in his photograph, and it was easy to peg him for military by his posture and athletic build. There was no fat anywhere on that man. His hair was longer than it was in his DMV picture, and it was a light brown that had lighter streaks running through it. He pulled out a head wrap similar to Jack's and pulled it down over his head.

There was an exuberance that radiated from Adam Taylor. It shone in his eyes and his smile. It made him look younger. I knew from his file he was twenty-nine and had served honorably in the navy for the past ten years. He was the boy next door, sculpted cheeks and crystalline blue eyes, and there was the slightest hint of a dimple in his chin.

"I've heard all about you from Vaughn," Adam said. "You must be a great guy. I'd be jealous if I didn't know you were married."

I decided it was a good time to insert myself into the conversation. I could've sworn I saw Vaughn blush, and I wasn't sure what was going on in Jack's mind.

"Hi," I said, moving in next to Jack and putting my arm around him. We were never much for public displays of affection, but I felt the need to align myself with Jack for Vaughn's sake. Maybe we were both overprotective after how devastated Vaughn had been after Daniel's murder.

"I'm J.J. Graves," I told Adam.

"Yes, Dr. Graves," he said, shaking my hand warmly. "I've heard all about you too."

"Oh, well..." I said, my smile strained as I tried to think which horrible things about my life Vaughn had chosen to share with him.

Adam leaned in and whispered, "Hey, you can't pick your family, right? I'll tell you all about mine someday over drinks. I promise it'll make you feel better."

I couldn't help but smile. He had that kind of contagious personality, and I could see why Vaughn liked him.

"I'd like that," I said.

"You coming on the ride?" Adam asked.

"Definitely not," I said. "I'm just dropping Jack off before I head over to the funeral home."

His smile disappeared. "It was terrible what happened to Brett yesterday. It really makes you think about how vulnerable you are out there, especially alone. But once you get that taste of freedom, the risk becomes worth it."

"Did you know Brett well?" I asked.

"About as well as any of us know each other," he said. "It's mostly casual friendships that develop here. Everyone loves to ride, so we have that in common. I can't say that Brett was really close to anyone though. Maybe Ginny. They talked a lot. But I don't know if Brett had a guy he'd go have a beer with or something. Know what I mean? He never came with us when we'd meet up for a drink after a ride somewhere."

"Who's Ginny?" I asked. I vaguely remembered her photograph from the night before, but nothing really stood out in my mind other than Jack saying she'd been a member of the club when he'd ridden before.

"She's over there talking to Benji," Adam said. "Come to think of it, I think maybe Benji and Brett might have gone out a time or two. I think they're in the same business or something. They were always talking about the stock market." Adam looked at Jack and said, "Glad to have you on the ride. Hope you can keep up." He slapped Jack on the shoulder and then took off toward the bike that was resting against the back of a tan Jeep.

"Wow," I said, pursing my lips at Vaughn. "He has a lot of…energy."

Vaughn laughed out loud, and it was nice to hear the sound, but Jack brought us back to the task at hand.

"Was Ginny making moves on Brett?" Jack asked.

"She sure gave it her best shot," Vaughn said.

I peeked around Vaughn's shoulder to get a glimpse of the woman in question. She was still talking to Benji Lyles, and it looked like whatever they were discussing was pretty serious.

She must have had a bad day at the DMV because that picture didn't do her justice. She was built, and spandex was clearly her friend because it defined everything and left nothing to the imagination. Her bright red hair was braided down her back and framed an alabaster face with the most perfect nose I'd ever seen and full lips that were made for nothing but sin.

"And did Brett reciprocate?" I asked.

"Nope," Vaughn said. "And she was not happy about it. You know how she is."

I arched a brow at that and gave Jack a look, but he avoided my gaze. "I don't know how she is," I said. "Maybe you could fill me in."

"She's always on the prowl," Jack said. "And she likes to get her way. Men are a challenge to her. The more married, the bigger the challenge. She can pour on the charm when she wants, and when she doesn't want to its best to stay in the clear. As long as you don't get attached she's basically harmless."

"Unless Brett rejected her and she went crazy and decided to kill him," I said. "Lord have mercy." At some point in our life together I'd love to stop coming face to face with the women Jack had had a relationship with.

Vaughn covered his laugh with a cough.

"What about the guy she's with?" I asked. "Benji Lyles. He's got a twenty-year-old cocaine conviction and a career in finance. Between Brett's rejection of Ginny and whatever he and Benji had to talk about when they went out together, it seems like they might have something to hide about our victim. Not to mention they don't look too happy with each other at the moment."

Jack sighed. "Well then, let's go talk to them and find out. But if she tries to take a bite out of me you'd better step in. I can't punch a woman this close to the election."

"You reap what you sow, my friend," I said. "But I'm happy to run interference for you. I've got my Taser if she gets fresh."

"Oh, that'll go over much better in the press."

"I thought so," I said, smiling.

12

JACK AND I MADE OUR WAY TOWARD GINNY AND Benji, but the sound of an air horn had everyone coming to attention and covering their ears. I looked around to see if I could find the offender and noticed Mitch Padgett standing on the bed of a pickup truck. He had a bullhorn in his hand.

"Seriously," I whispered to Jack. "He's that guy. I'm surprised nobody has knocked his caps off."

"Why do you think he has the caps?" Jack murmured between closed lips.

My ears rang from the air horn, but it had done the trick. I didn't hear one clatter of shoes or a whisper. Though that could've have been because of temporary deafness.

"Friends and fellow cyclists," Mitch said.

"Oh, for Pete's sake," I whispered.

"Thank you for showing your dedication to honor our friend, Brett Jorgenson. Brett was taken much too soon, but he died doing what he loved. It's a risk we all take, and I can't think of a better way to go."

"I can," I said so only Jack could hear me. "This guy is a lunatic."

"Ssh," Jack said, but I could feel his shoulders shaking with laughter beside me.

"So today," Mitch continued, "we ride for Brett. We ride for all of us. Give it everything you've got, and be safe out there. The Cardinals are going to kick us off, and then a team will depart every ten minutes. The Old Dominions will ride last and bring it home for Brett."

There was a cheer from the group and people scattered to get their bikes and move to the road. The Old Dominion team shifted to the side and got out of the way as the other teams prepared. Ginny and Benji hadn't moved from where they'd stood, but they were no longer in a heated conversation.

Jack took me by the elbow and maneuvered me through the crowd until we were standing in front of them.

Ginny's full lips tilted in a wicked smile, and I found even I was mesmerized by her appeal. A mere man wouldn't stand a chance against that. Brett Jorgenson must have been a saint.

"Well, if it isn't Jack Lawson in the flesh," she purred. Her voice was Southern and sultry, and I fought the urge to roll my eyes. "I thought that was you over there. I didn't realize you'd come for a…ride."

The double entendre was so obvious Jack started laughing, which was clearly the wrong thing to do. Ginny's eyes went hard like green lasers, and she propped a hand on a voluptuous hip.

Jack held out his hand to Benji and introduced himself. "Jack Lawson," he said.

"Benji Lyles." He shook Jack's hand and said, "You used to ride with the club?"

"Several years ago before the job got in the way," Jack said. "What about you? How long have you been riding?"

"About a year and a half," he said. "It was actually Brett who got me to join the group."

"Oh yeah?" Jack asked. "Y'all work together?"

Benji laughed. "I wish," he said. "We're both in finance, but I'm nowhere in his league. He's big time. I own the Edward Jones in King George. I'd give you a card, but they're in my car."

"Geez, Benji," Ginny said, shaking her head. "Did you learn nothing from your jailbird past? The cops don't just show up for no reason, and here you are vomiting your business."

Benji didn't seem to be shaken about her comment and he just smiled a little sheepishly. "My misspent youth," he confided. "Just stupid kid stuff. I was in the wrong place at the wrong time with the wrong people. I was at Harvard on full scholarship, and expensive drugs were part of life. Except that my parents were poor and had no strings to pull when we got busted. So I lost my scholarship, got kicked out, and ended up with a felony on my record. Almost wrecked my whole life. Maybe if I'd done things differently it'd be me sitting in a high-rise office on Wall Street instead of in a strip mall in King George."

There didn't seem to be any bitterness in the statement. He'd seemed to accept it as part of his life and moved on.

"You and Brett were friends?" I asked.

"Brett wasn't really friends with anyone," Ginny said. "He kept himself separated. Kind of high and mighty."

"Be nice, Ginny," Benji scolded. "Just because he didn't give you the time of day doesn't mean he wasn't friendly. We went out a couple of times to grab lunch after a Saturday ride. He was just really introverted, so it seemed like he didn't really interact with the group, but he was a really nice guy. I asked if he'd mind giving me a couple of tips for the business, and he took the time to share a few things with me. He helped me open up my client base and he really helped steer me in the right direction as far as investments are concerned."

"He seemed okay on the Thursday ride?" Jack asked. "Nothing was bothering him?"

Benji shrugged. "Not that I could tell. Brett wasn't really one of those guys who are real expressive. The only thing I ever saw him worry much about was his wife. She had some early labor issues a couple of months back, so he missed some rides while they were getting her stabilized, but everything was fine after that. The group sent her a get-well basket. He seemed real appreciative that we'd think about them."

Ginny's eyes had sharpened when Jack started asking questions. "I thought Floyd Parker was the one who hit Brett yesterday," she said. "That news spread faster than if the paper had printed it. Convenient for you, huh? I heard things weren't going so well in the Lawson camp."

"Death is never convenient," Jack told her evenly.

"You're such a bitch, Ginny," Benji said. "Brett's dead. What's even your purpose in life other than trying to make people miserable who don't succumb to your will? How many good men have you run off from this group and how many marriages have you tried to ruin because you're a miserable dried-up shell of a woman? Your beauty is only going to last so long. Bitterness and anger has aged you. I regret sleeping with you every day."

Ginny squared off with Benji and said snottily, "Your therapy is showing."

"I'm okay with that," he said. "You should try it."

I pressed my lips together and Jack and I slowly backed away. They weren't paying attention to us anyway, but now I understood why the tension had been so high between Ginny and Benji.

"What do you think?" I asked him.

"I think he's right," Jack said. "Therapy would do her a lot of good. I haven't seen her in years. She didn't used to be like that."

"Brett rejects her and she decides if she can't have him, no one will?" I asked.

"Or maybe Benji was lying about Brett helping him," Jack said. "The stock market is a brutal business. Maybe Brett gave him bad advice and he killed him for revenge."

"I like my theory better," I said. I took out my phone and looked at our list. "You've still a possible connection between Brett and Morgan. He retired earlier this year from banking. Shara Woosley is a CPA, and Kendra Beatty is an actuary for a large insurance company. They all are or were in finance, but it seems like a smaller scale than what Brett was used to dealing with. But there's Mario Ricci." I nodded toward the swarthy-looking man talking to Vaughn. "He's a hedge fund manager. He might be more in Brett's circle of things."

"Maybe," Jack said. "Have you noticed that woman keeps looking at us?"

"What woman?" I asked, turning my head, but Jack put his hands on each side of my face and leaned down to kiss me.

"Settle down, Captain Obvious," he said. "Caucasian female. About five ten. Dark blond hair. Looks like the Queen of the Amazons."

I snorted a laugh at the description. "Yeah, that's Leslie Carron," I said. "I don't think she's a fan of yours. She wasn't too happy when Mitch was singing your praises."

"Yeah, I noticed that," he said. "Leslie Carron. I know that name from somewhere, but I'm not sure where I've heard it. It'll come to me eventually."

"Maybe in the meantime stay out of her way," I said. "Who knew the bike club had such dangerous women?"

"It's a group of thrill seekers," Jack said. "What did you expect? We're about to head out." He handed me the keys to the truck. "I'm going to unload my bike and get ready. Be careful leaving the parking lot. I'll have Vaughn swing me back to the station when we're done."

"I'm going to find Cole and get those samples from the water bottles and see if they can pull any prints."

We knuckle bumped and headed off to our respective corners, and I passed by Vaughn on the way to the truck. He was straddling a familiar-looking bike and pressing buttons on his Garmin. I knew that bike. I'd been staring at pictures of it for the last two days.

"Hey," I said. "You and Brett Jorgenson have the same bike?"

"Yeah," Vaughn said, his smiling face going sober. "I really like Brett's. We're a similar size so he let me try it out. I finally put one on order a couple of months back, and it came in this week."

I didn't know why that bit of information bothered me, but for some reason, it did. I wished Vaughn a safe ride and then got in the truck. The sky was just starting to turn gray, so I waited until the last cyclist had left the parking lot before I finally pulled out.

I had more questions than answers at this point, but there was one thing I felt very positive about—I'd already met Brett Jorgenson's killer.

13

I CALLED COLE ON THE WAY INTO THE STATION SO he'd know I was on the way in, and I watched the town wake up as the sun rose. I rolled the window down and breathed in the cold morning air, and I felt peace wash over me. I'd learned that peace wasn't the absence of chaos. There was chaos all around us, but Jack was my center, and as long as my center was in alignment, everything else fell into place.

Business around the square was back to normal. There were displays set out on the sidewalks and chalk signs with clever sayings. Someone had fixed the scarecrow display and uprighted the pumpkins and hay bales. I smiled when I passed a giant sign in front of the courthouse that said *Re-Elect Jack Lawson for Sheriff*.

There was plenty of parking in front of the sheriff's office since there was about to be a shift change. Cole was waiting for me by the front entrance.

"Don't usually see you this early in the morning," Cole said teasingly.

"Jack decided it was a good time to dust off his cycling shoes," I said. "Apparently, there are a lot of people who like to ride bicycles in the dark in freezing temperatures."

"Savages," Cole said, shuddering. "Anything new on the Jorgenson case from your end? Jack sent me all the backgrounds of the guys you ran last night."

This was the tricky part of working with Carver. Technically, any information he dug out for us was a favor. An undetected favor. We knew we were blessed with Carver's friendship and his resources. It made our jobs much easier. But we couldn't use any of the information he came up with in an official capacity. We could only take that information and put pressure on suspects to reveal more evidence or confess.

"We talked to a few interesting characters this morning," I told him. "And there are a couple of standouts. Poison is typically a woman's murder weapon of choice. It's not so messy. And there's a woman in the bike club who pursued the victim pretty hot and heavy, but he rejected her for his wife."

"A woman scorned…" he said.

"Exactly," I said. "But I don't know. I don't like her, but I'm not sure she'd be our killer. There are several people in that group who could have potential motive, but from everything we've seen, Brett Jorgenson was truly a stand-up guy. He helped people in his field when that business is typically cutthroat. He was loyal to his wife and his family. It's like when he made the switch from his former life of drug use and high living, he *really* made the switch. This whole thing is just weird. I can't see a motive behind killing Brett Jorgenson." Unless something major comes up in the financials Carver was digging into, I added silently.

"Maybe we'll get lucky with a fingerprint," Cole said. "Sergeant Morgenstern is going to meet us at evidence lockup. He's the best at pulling prints. Maybe we'll get lucky."

"We could use a little of that right now," I said.

"There's a lot of enthusiasm about the election," Cole said. "I wouldn't worry too much about how it's going to go at the polls. I know Jack has been under a lot of pressure to give the green light on those prisons, but Jack does a good job of listening to the community. And most of the community is against it."

"Most," I said. "But not all. I don't really keep up with a lot of the politics happening in the county. Maybe I should. But I think it would mostly give me a headache and make me want to move."

Cole snorted. "Politics has a tendency to make people feel that way. It's never as simple as it should be. But King George is prime real estate that's mostly undeveloped, and it's within proximity of major cities. The pressure was amped up earlier this year when AvantGuard moved their headquarters to King George Proper."

"AvantGuard," I said. "Why does that sound familiar?"

"They're a private security contractor for the government," he said. "We're talking big money. And they're very much in favor of the prisons being built here, and they're happy to throw money behind candidates and make promises to anyone they can to see it happen."

"I had no idea they'd moved here," I said. "There was nothing in the media. And Jack never mentioned it."

"No, he wouldn't," Cole said. "But it's a new headache to worry about. They'd started buying up land to build their new headquarters on the down low. They were very patient, picking it up here and there until they had what they needed, and then all of a sudden building started taking place for their facility."

There were so many moving parts to Jack's job. It was never just law and order. It was taxes and politics and zoning and all the daily minutiae that would make me crazy but that made Jack thrive.

Evidence lockup was in the far corner of the building, and I'd only been there one other time. Mostly because it was creepy. The lights flickered and the hallway was dark and narrow. I felt bad for whoever was assigned to duty. It wasn't the most ideal working condition.

Evidence lockup was floor-to-ceiling chain-link with an area cut out for a counter and login sheet. There was an older man sitting behind the chest-high counter reading the newspaper, his glasses perched on the end of his nose as he read. His hair was like a white cloud on his head and there were tufts of wiry gray hair coming from his ears.

"Hey, Bradley," Cole said as we approached the counter.

Bradley squinted above his glasses and then his wide face stretched into a grin. "Detective Cole," he said. "Long time, no see. Who's the pretty lady?"

I'd never met Deputy Bradley before, but I'd certainly heard stories about him. He was in his seventies, and he was one of those men who couldn't let go of the job. He was way past his prime but refused to retire. He didn't seem to mind sitting behind a desk and locked away in the bowels of the department as long as he got to put on the uniform every day.

"This is Dr. Graves," Cole said. "The sheriff's wife."

I wasn't sure why he'd added the last part. Most people knew who I was, and if they didn't we never bothered to explain. So it made me wonder why Cole felt it was necessary.

Bradley turned his pale blue gaze to me and his bushy eyebrows rose in surprise. "Oh, is she now," he said.

But Cole didn't bother to let him think on it too long. "I'm here to pick up the evidence bag from the Jorgenson case."

"Oh, sure, sure," Bradley said. "I got it right here. Barely had time to process it."

Bradley hefted his bulk out of a black cushy chair and made his way to a table that had a large evidence bag. He grabbed the bag and then waddled back to us.

"You just gotta sign it out," Bradley said. He pushed a clipboard across the counter to Cole, and Cole scrawled his signature.

"It's all yours," Bradley said. Then he looked at me shrewdly. "Sure hope the sheriff can pull it out for this election. Lots of people seem to think we need some new blood in here."

I arched a brow, not 100 percent sure what I thought about Bradley. Jack didn't seem to care for him, though he'd never really said what kind of cop he'd been when he was out on the street. But I understood Bradley served a purpose. Not every cop that was hired was going to rise through the ranks or even try to be anything more than adequate at the job. There were always those content to show up and get a paycheck and do nothing more. Those people tended to get shuffled around until they were put in a position where they were generally forgotten. Like Bradley.

"I'm not too worried about it," I said. "The people in this county are smart enough to know that sometimes new blood brings nothing but diseases."

Bradley harrumphed and Cole and I headed back down the long hallway. I could feel Bradley's eyes on us until we were out of sight.

"That guy is creepy," I said.

"Bradley?" Cole asked. "He's harmless. Just stubborn. He wasn't happy when Jack was elected and the old sheriff got booted out. He should've taken retirement, but he's not the kind of guy anyone listens to so Jack wasn't worried about him trying to be divisive. It was easier just to send him back here and forget about him. Bradley vowed to die behind the badge. A guy like that wouldn't know what to do with himself if he became a civilian. He'd probably end up eating a bullet."

"Lovely thought," I said.

"It happens more often than you know," Cole said. "Come on, Morgenstern is going to meet us in the conference room. He should have everything set up in there. You've got everything you need?"

I patted my medical bag. "I'm just doing a swab of the inside of the bottles and then I'll take everything back to the lab. I have the tox screen to compare the sample to, so it shouldn't take too long. But I've got to send it to the lab in Richmond to get a specific lock on the amphetamines. It could be anything from street cut to a prescription."

"Aren't some of the riders in the club doctors?"

"Yes," I told him. "But I can't imagine any of the people I met today risking having their license pulled for a fake prescription. They've all been established in their careers here in King George for a long time. They'd lose everything. And for what? What would their motive be?"

Cole blew out a breath. "I guess that's our job to find out."

Sergeant Morgenstern was a stocky man somewhere in his mid-forties. He had a square head and square body, and his once-dark hair had turned salt-and-pepper gray. He had brown puppy dog eyes that showed intelligence, and the gold wedding ring on his finger looked tight and as if it had been there a long time.

I'd known Morgenstern a while. He was in charge of the forensics team that came to crime scenes to collect evidence, so our paths crossed frequently, but we rarely had reason to interact.

"Hey, Doc," he said, nodding to me when I came into the conference room ahead of Cole.

"Morgenstern," I said. "How's it going?"

"Can't complain," he said, continuing to set up his fingerprinting kit. He put on a pair of gloves and then took the bag from Cole. He opened it and took out the two water bottles.

I hadn't paid much attention to the water bottles when I'd been standing over Brett Jorgenson's body on the side of the road. But now that I looked at them there was something niggling in the back of my mind that bothered me.

"What is it?" Cole asked, staring at me.

"Man, I really need to work on my poker face," I said.

"Understatement," Cole said. "But to be fair, you have gotten a lot better at it."

"I appreciate that," I said dryly. "There's just something in my gut that's not sitting right. When I was at the ride this morning, I noticed everyone riding for Old Dominion had these same water bottles. And Vaughn and Brett Jorgenson have the exact same bicycle."

Cole raised his brows at that. "You think Brett wasn't the intended victim?"

"I don't know," I said. "It's just a thought. We just haven't found anything that pops yet for why Brett would be a target. But I can think of even less of a reason for Vaughn to be a target."

"You want to go ahead and get your swab?" Morgenstern asked.

"Yeah, if you don't mind," I said, pulling on my own gloves. "No matter how hard I try I can never manage to escape without getting black powder all over me."

"Believe me," Morgenstern said, "my wife feels your pain. I have to change clothes in the mudroom and put my things in a bag before she'll let me come in the house."

I took several long swabs from my bag and then swiped the remaining contents of the inside of the water bottles. They'd both been empty when we'd found the victim, so whatever had been inside, he drunk all of it.

I noticed the cotton at the end of the swabs was tinged red when I pulled it out, but I figured I could ask Jack. I wanted to get back to the lab.

I used a pair of scissors to cut off the tips of the swabs, and Cole held a sterile bag open for me so they could drop inside. I sealed the bag and stripped off my gloves.

"That should do it," I said. And then I looked at Morgenstern. "Good luck. We could sure use a break on this one."

"No pressure," he said, giving me a not-optimistic smile.

"I'll let you know if we get a hit," Cole said.

I nodded and made my way back out from the way I'd come. But there was something unsettled in my gut that this crime wasn't exactly as it seemed.

14

I'D GOTTEN COMPLACENT OVER THE LAST TWENTY-four hours, thinking my life and position had been forgotten. But when I pulled onto Catherine of Aragon I saw the reporters camped out on the street.

Floyd and the accident should have been the story, taking up headline space, but for some reason they seemed fixed on me and my reaction to the bomb-shell earlier in the week. I pulled under the carport and got all my things together before opening the door and heading up the ramp quickly.

There was a white van and an older model green SUV. There was a camera crew and a blond woman dressed in a red power suit.

"Dr. Graves," she called out. "Do you have any comments about your husband fathering a secret child? Do you think it'll cost him the election? Have you filed for divorce? Do you still plan to charge

Floyd Parker with vehicular manslaughter while knowing that someone else murdered Brett Jorgenson? Are you and your husband using your positions to take revenge on his opponent?"

My teeth were grinding together by the time I reached the door and got the key in the lock, and I could still hear her pounding out questions when I finally closed the door behind me. I guessed that was Floyd's advantage of working for the paper. But what I really wanted to know was who had leaked the information that Brett Jorgenson had been murdered. I hadn't yet released the autopsy findings to Floyd's attorney. And the only people who knew what Jack and I knew were supposedly the ones working the case.

I made sure to lock the door and set the alarm behind me, and then I headed down to the lab. I felt the urgency pressing against me. It wouldn't take me long to run tests and make a match to what was found in Brett Jorgenson's tox screen.

I started the process and was waiting for results when my cell rang. I could hear it ringing, but I couldn't remember where I'd put it in my rush to get from the car to inside the funeral home.

I checked my pockets and dug in my bag, but then I saw the paper vibrating on my desk and realized I'd set papers on top of it in my hurry. It was Jack.

"Hey," I said by way of greeting. "I'm just finishing up here now. I should have swab results any minute."

"Good," Jack said. "Would you mind bringing the truck and picking us up? Vaughn had a tire blow out and I stopped with him. We're on the side of the highway. He took a pretty nasty spill."

I took down the directions to their location and said, "I'm on the way."

————

I'D BEEN WORRIED the reporters would try to follow me, but I had nothing to worry about. They were gone when I came back out of the funeral home, less than two hours after I'd entered.

Jack had said Vaughn's tire had blown over by the state park, so I turned onto Anne Boleyn and then hit the highway since it was faster than the back roads. I had my medical kit in case Vaughn needed attention, and I had the results of the swab test. I still hadn't heard anything from Cole about fingerprints.

It took me almost half an hour to get to their location. Jack said they'd taken their bikes off the road about half a mile from a roadside vegetable stand. I passed the stand and a few cars that had stopped to see what the farmer had to offer, and I slowed down, looking for their bikes.

Jack was waiting for me and flagged me down, and I pulled to the side of the road and hit the hazard lights.

"Everybody okay?" I asked when I got out.

"He's just got some bumps and bruises," Jack said. "And he's fairly pissed off. That bike is only a week old."

"Yeah, he told me," I said, wincing in sympathy.

We walked over to where Vaughn was sitting on the grass. Both of his elbows were bloody and there was a good-sized tear on his leg warmers exposing a bloody knee. Other than that, he looked okay at first glance. But Jack was right. He was definitely pissed.

I'd learned enough growing up with boys that pride and ego were almost always at stake, so I checked him over silently while he fumed.

"I can clean you up better at the house," I said. Jack was already loading up the bikes in the rack. "Besides, I figure you could probably use a beer while I kiss your boo-boos."

He gave me a look and I winked at him. And then I gave him a hand up.

"I'd rather just go home," he said.

"I know, cowboy," I said. "But we don't always get our way. Unless you're waiting for a tall, dark, and handsome sailor to come by and rescue you."

Vaughn's cheeks turned crimson. "How'd you know he was in the navy?"

I kept my head down as I navigated us across the ditch and to the truck so Vaughn couldn't see my face as I lied. "He was wearing his dog tags this morning."

Vaughn seemed satisfied with that answer, and we all piled into the truck. I got behind the wheel since Jack was still wearing his cycling shoes.

"So what happened?" I asked.

"I must have hit a rock or something," Vaughn said. "Those tires are rail thin and at 135psi. It doesn't take much for them to blow. I've just never had one blow quite like that. Normally, I'd just change out the tire and keep riding, but it bent my rim."

"You're lucky it didn't bend your face," I said.

"This face has a guardian angel," Vaughn said. "It'd be a crime to mess with this kind of perfection."

I rolled my eyes but was glad to see he was in better spirits.

"It's actually rather fortuitous that this happened," he said. "Now I can pin both of you down and go over some final election issues. Maybe we should call your mother to come over too. We've been trying to pin you down for weeks, but you're slippery. And before you can argue, I've already made up my mind you're not going to get rid of me. I'm going to recover in your wonderful sauna and soak my sore muscles in your hot tub."

"It's an election," Jack said. "People donate money and it's your job to spend it how you see fit. That's why you're in charge of that stuff. And my mother is in charge of getting people to donate the money you're in charge of. Why don't the two of you have a meeting and leave me out of it?"

"Oh, we have been," Vaughn said. "Hey, it's the least you can do for me. I was supposed to spend the afternoon sailing."

"With anyone we know?" I asked nosily.

"Maybe," he said. "So you owe me."

"Fine," Jack said. "Call my mother. Make a party of it. But we still have a pesky murder to solve."

"Yes," he said. "I've been a huge help in that area too. I truly don't know what you'd do without me."

When we got back to the house, I helped Vaughn inside while Jack took care of the bikes. I pointed him to a barstool, cleaned his wounds, and then gave him an ice pack for his knee which had pretty significant swelling. By the time Jack came in, Vaughn's wounds were tended to and he was nursing a beer.

"Y'all any closer to finding who killed Brett?" he asked.

"I don't know if closer is the right word," I said. "But the residue from the inside of his water bottles is a match with the amphetamines that came back in Brett's tox screen. I'm going to send everything off to the lab in Richmond and see if they can give me something more specific on the amphetamines. I did notice my swabs came back red when I pulled them out. Any reason for that?"

"Electrolytes," Vaughn and Jack said together.

And then Jack said, "Everyone has their own concoction they use for rides. Gatorade powder, electrolyte tabs, things like that. You hear back from Cole on whether they found prints on the bottles?"

"Not yet," I said. "And I assume you haven't heard from Carver."

"Well, then," Vaughn said. "I'm going to soak and call your mother. It sounds like the perfect time to do non-murdery things."

"You'd think that," Jack said, pressing his lips together.

I waited until Vaughn had taken off to the back of the house where the sauna and hot tub were located, and then said, "I need to talk to you."

"Come upstairs," he said. "I need to change anyway."

He grabbed a couple of bottles of water and I followed him upstairs to our bedroom. He stripped down and turned on the shower.

"What's going on?" he asked.

"I don't know," I said. "Just a feeling."

"Feelings are legitimate," he said. "What kind of feelings?"

"I'm not sure Brett was the target or that he was meant to die," I said.

Jack sat down on the edge of the tub and drank a full bottle of water. "Because there's no clear motive?" he asked.

"Among other things," I said. "Did you notice Brett and Vaughn have the same bike? He said he just got it this week."

Jack nodded. "And it would've been easy to mix up water bottles and bicycles, especially if someone didn't realize Vaughn had gotten a new bike. But what would be a motive for killing Vaughn?"

"I'm not sure it would have killed him," I said. "Vaughn is healthy with healthy organs. He probably would have passed out or gotten lightheaded or crashed. But he probably wouldn't have died."

Jack was silent for a few minutes while he thought it through. "I don't know," he said. "It's something to consider, but we do have some threads to pull with the Old Dominion members. We know for certain it had to be someone on Thursday's ride who spiked the water and replaced the bottles, accident or not."

"What about Vaughn's bike today?" I asked. "Any chance that wasn't an accident?"

Jack's mouth pressed into a hard line and he got into the shower. "There's always a chance. I'll look at the bike and see if I can see signs of sabotage. We need to call Carver and have him run some new probabilities. I'm about tired of the people I love being targeted."

15

I WAS SURPRISED TO SEE JACK'S MOM APPEAR ON the doorbell app on my phone, and I hurried down the stairs to let her in while Jack was still changing.

I opened the door and she threw her arms around me. "There's my girl," she said. "I'm glad to see you home. My son is a moron. I take full responsibility. But I can see he took my advice and crawled across broken glass to get you back."

My lips twitched and I said, "something like that."

"Good for you. He needs to suffer a little bit," she said, winking. "He always did have it too easy in life. But don't make him suffer too much. He's still my son, and moron or not, I love him. Though if he makes me lose my favorite daughter I warned him I was going to pick you."

She hugged me again and then scurried into the kitchen. I'd never seen Jeri Lawson do anything slow. She was a hundred miles an hour all the time, and had more energy in her tiny body than I could even comprehend.

"You look tired," she said, heading into the kitchen. I followed behind her and watched with interest as she sat on one of the bar stools and then immediately got up again to move around the kitchen. "I'm sure you haven't been getting any sleep with all that Floyd Parker nonsense. His mother should have drowned him at birth. He's never been anything but a snot-nosed brat who caused trouble everywhere he went. There's no way he's going to pull off a win on Tuesday."

She went to the refrigerator and pantry and started getting out things to make sandwiches.

"Is everything okay?" I asked.

And then to my surprise and horror, she burst into tears.

"Ohmigosh," I said, looking around to see if someone was going to swoop in and tell me what the heck was going on. "Are you okay? Are you hurt?"

I'd known Jack's mom almost as long as I'd known my own mother, and I certainly knew her better than my own mother. But in all my life I could never remember seeing her cry. I went to her and put my arm around her, and she leaned in for a minute. But she wasn't the kind of woman who liked to lean on anyone for very long.

"I'm fine, I'm fine," she said, pulling away and tearing a paper towel from the roll to blow her nose.

"It's been a difficult week," she said. "As you know. But I guess the call I got this morning was just the icing on the cake. I received a visit from the board of directors of the club yesterday. Apparently, a member had complained about my use of the facility for private fundraisers for Jack's campaign. Of course, this has never been an issue before and it states in our bylaws that members can use the facility for events." She waved her hand dismissively. "Anyway, I told them to tell whoever complained to shove it where the sun don't shine. I know who it is, and she hasn't been a member that long, but she's a pain in the behind coming in and wanting to change things and throwing money around to get her way. We've been members in that club for thirty years. The board seemed apologetic when they left my house yesterday. But the board president came back today by himself and told me Rich and my membership had been revoked and the watch party and celebration we had scheduled in the ballroom for Tuesday night has been cancelled."

She started crying again just as Jack walked in. He gave me a questioning look, but I just shook my head as he went over to wrap her in his arms.

"It just doesn't make any sense," she said. "They said I was breaking the bylaws and all this other nonsense, but I helped write those bylaws. I can't believe they'd just kick us out after all the money we've donated and everything else we've done for them. I'm a committee head for Pete's sake. There is something dirty going on here and I'm going to find out what it is. Either that, or I'm going to burn the whole place to the ground."

Jack winced. "Let's maybe hold off on that option for a bit. But you're right. Something isn't right. You and dad know all of the board members. Have you called and tried talking to them to see what's going on?"

"They're dodging our calls," she said. "Your dad dropped me off here and said he was hunting board members. He said he'd hang their heads on the wall of his office with the animals. You know nothing much ruffles your dad, but it makes him mad when people make me cry."

Vaughn came in at that moment and said, "There's my girl." And then he stopped in his tracks when he saw Jeri's tear-streaked face. "What did y'all do to her?"

"We didn't do anything, thank you very much," Jack said.

Vaughn scoffed. "Don't say that as if there's no reason to assume. You didn't even tell your mother she was a grandma."

Jeri started crying harder at that and Jack took a step toward Vaughn, but Vaughn stood his ground.

"Hey man, don't take your own screwups out on me," Vaughn said.

"It's not your business, and it's not your place," Jack said calmly. "I know you're mad. And you've got every right to be. Hell, everyone has a right to be angry at me after this week. I own it and I know it. But you're the bottom of the totem pole here, so back off."

Vaughn blew out a breath and took a step back. "Fine," he said. "You're right. I'm sorry." Then he turned his attention to Jeri and spoke gently. "What happened, love?"

Vaughn had that way about him that could make strong people melt, and Jeri turned into his arms and let him hold her while she explained what had happened.

"We don't need them," Vaughn said. "It's just dirty politics. There are some new people in this county who have money and are trying to use it to get Jack out of office, but we're not going to let them do it. We've got friends in high places too, and it's time to use them. I'm going to call Marco Lombardi and see if we can use his restaurant for the victory party. He's got that big space out back where we can put up a tent with a stage and lights. It'll be even better than the country club."

Jeri lifted her head, a stubborn line creased on her forehead, and she nodded. "You're right. That stupid board of directors is going to rue the day they messed with my family. Maybe we should start our own exclusive club. Jack, you should buy up some land and build a golf course."

"I'll get right on that," Jack said dryly. "I do appreciate you both. I know running a campaign isn't easy, and I couldn't do it without you. Mostly because I have no desire to do it." He grinned and handed me his phone so I could read the text that just came in. "But I know it's a necessary job so I can do *this* job. Thanks for believing in me."

I read the text twice to make sure it was correct. Morgenstern had found a partial print on the cap of one of the water bottles and a full thumbprint. And a match hadn't taken long because the prints were already in the system.

"I can see by the look on Jaye's face that y'all are going to have to go do murder stuff," Vaughn said. "But let me tell you the money doesn't lie. The people in this county are funding your campaign and you still have more than a million dollars in the war chest. But Floyd's money is coming from an outside donor. So don't let all of this stuff that's happening play mind games. He tried to knock you off with the story in the paper and then this thing with the country club. He's trying to keep everything in your life and the people in it in an upheaval. Don't let him do it."

Jack looked at me and I could practically read his mind. Upheaval was the right word. And would whoever was pulling the strings attempt murder to continue the chaos? Was this all about Jack?

I felt guilty for not telling Vaughn where we were going. I busied myself gathering my things while Jack finished up business. Vaughn would be able to tell something was wrong if he saw my face. We said quick goodbyes and headed out, this time taking the Tahoe.

Jack waited until we were on the road before he called Cole. "Can you send me the home address for Adam Taylor?"

"Doing it now," Cole said. "You think he's the guy?"

"I think he's definitely a guy worth talking to," Jack said. "They might still be out on the ride. I'm going to swing by Vaughn's place and see if we can head him off."

"It's always too good to be true," I said. "Poor Vaughn."

Jack headed toward King George Proper and the vitamin shop. We passed cyclists on the way who were finishing up their ride. When we arrived, there were fewer cars than there had been earlier that morning, but it looked like there were still a couple of teams out. Several cyclists were in the parking lot in stages of undress or in conversation.

"Vaughn said Adam Taylor had a Jeep," I said, pointing to the sand-colored hardtop in the end parking spot on the farthest row.

"That's his," Jack said. "Vaughn rode in with him this morning. I saw him get in and get some of his stuff before we took off."

"When Vaughn was talking about the lives of the people you love being thrown into chaos this week," I said, "he didn't mention himself. He's got a bike exactly like our victim and then today that new bike has a blowout. And the guy he's been riding with, who has access to his bike, left his fingerprints on the water bottles with the amphetamines in them."

"There's no such thing as a coincidence in an investigation," Jack said. "But right now even fingerprints would be circumstantial. You saw how chaotic things were before the ride this morning. Everyone's bottles are the same. But I agree with you. I don't think this has anything to do with Brett Jorgenson."

Jack pulled into a parking space that faced Adam Taylor's Jeep. "We passed several of the Old Dominion riders on the way here," he said. "We shouldn't have to wait too long before he shows up." The phone rang and Carver's name came up on the screen. "Tell me you've got good news, Carver."

"I certainly have interesting news," Carver said. "But I don't know if it's helpful. I didn't find anything unusual on the financial side of things.

None of these guys are in major debt. Their businesses are doing well. And there are no iffy or hidden accounts that I can find. Believe me, I looked hard.

"When I didn't find anything in financial records I started going through medical records. And I found one of the suspects on your list has a prescription for Adderall."

"The ADD drug?" Jack asked. "Why is that significant?"

"Because Adderall is an amphetamine," I said.

"Exactly," Carver said. "Normally it might not have stood out or even showed up in this level of search because it's so commonly prescribed, but in the military you have to have medical permission to get a prescription for Adderall. In fact, you have to have the drug out of your system for a year before you can even join the military, and then once you're enlisted you've got to go through a rigorous process to get put back on it. They keep a close watch on anyone who takes that kind of drug."

"Adam Taylor," Jack said.

"Bingo," Carver told him.

"We just found his fingerprints on Jorgenson's water bottles."

"You're going to need nothing short of a confession for this one," Carver said. "There's circumstantial evidence all over the place. An attorney would laugh at you."

"Yeah, I'm aware," Jack said.

"I also found out something else while I've been filling my free time with constructive and helpful things," Carver said.

Jack's lips twitched. "Oh, yeah? What's that?"

"AvantGuard should have better cybersecurity," he said.

"You didn't," Jack said, raising his brows and looking at me with concern. "They will kill you if they find out."

"Please," Carver said. "Like they'll find out. But you probably want to know what's going on right under your nose. They've been buying up property in King George like crazy, offering a lot of the farmers more than double what the land is worth. The good news is that the people in King George are stubborn and most have turned down the offers. But they bought out Floyd Parker's parents' place. About two hundred acres. And they're trying desperately to get the land adjacent to it."

"Let me guess," Jack said. "AvantGuard is one of the main investors in the private prisons they want to build here."

"Got it in one," Carver said. "But it's not the Avant-Guard name they're buying the property under. The main company is called Trident, and they own several corporations under that name in different fields. Real-estate development is one of them. They've done a good job layering the companies so it's hard to find out who is who and which company is buying up property. It's very much like a military operation. They're flanking King George County and about to make an attack. And you're the last person they're going to want as sheriff, because it's you who can make or break this deal."

"I think you're definitely onto something," Jack told Carver. "Let's start with Adam Taylor and see what layers we can peel back. He's got a lot of explaining to do."

16

WE DIDN'T HAVE TO WAIT LONG AFTER CARVER hung up for several of the Old Dominion riders to glide into the parking lot. It was hard to distinguish between them, with the exception of Ginny Grant. There was no mistaking her curves and red hair.

We watched Adam pull the cap from his head and drink deeply from his bottle, and then he unclipped his shoes and got off the bike. There was plenty of jovial conversation from the riders as they cooled down and got their bikes racked.

Ginny seemed to be in a particularly good mood as she unzipped her jersey and stripped down to her sports bra. But she wasn't alone as the other female rider in the group, Leslie Carron, did the same. Benji Lyles was with them and pointing out something along the rim of his tire to Adam. Everyone seemed in a good mood, and whatever bad blood had been between Benji and Ginny earlier that morning seemed to have disappeared.

"Do you think Vaughn's tire mishap this morning was accidental?" I asked Jack while we continued to watch them.

"I'm going to check the bike when we get back home," he said. "But it's not hard to sabotage a bike. The problem is those tires are so full that when they blow, they tend to shred. I might not be able to find any evidence it was tampered with. But if someone was trying to get Vaughn out of the way by spiking his drink and that didn't work, then why wouldn't they try again by tampering with his bike?"

They group was starting to part ways, tossing shoes and clothes into their cars and making sure their bikes were secure. I moved to open the door so we could intercept Adam before he left but Jack put his hand on my arm to stop me.

"Well," he said. "Will you look at that."

I maneuvered my body toward his side of the Tahoe so I could see exactly what he was looking at and gasped. "That jerk," I said. "How dare he pretend to be gay just so he can get to Vaughn."

The door to Adam's Jeep was open, and he leaned against the seat with his legs planted firmly on the ground. He was pelvis to pelvis with Leslie Carron. His hands rested on her hips and he smiled at whatever it was she was whispering in his ear. She finished it off with a quick nip to his earlobe and then she sashayed away to her black Lexus.

We weren't the only ones who'd noticed the exchange. Ginny and Benji both watched from the sidelines.

"Yikes," I said. "If looks could kill Adam would be dead."

Ginny's green gaze shot daggers at Leslie, and Benji looked like he wanted to do bodily harm to Adam.

"Gotta love the drama," Jack said. "It's just like a soap opera. Benji loves Leslie, she doesn't love anyone because she's an ice queen, but she does enjoy the opposite sex every now and again, and it's just a bonus if she can make Benji jealous or let others think she can make Adam play for her team. Ginny thinks every man should always pick her first. And Benji is grateful when anyone picks him at all."

"What's the story with Leslie?" I asked, smiling at Jack's rundown of the players. "She was the one giving you the dirty looks this morning while Mitch publicly threw his support to you."

"Oh, yeah," he said. "She's a weird one. Doesn't really seem like she fits in with the group, but she can obviously hang. More of an observer. I keep thinking she seems familiar, but I can't place her. She kind of blends in with the scenery."

"She's pretty in an understated way," I said. "But you're right. She tends to blend in, especially standing next to Ginny."

"Let's go," Jack said, letting go of my arm, and we got out of the Tahoe.

Adam didn't see us until we were almost to the Jeep, and then he turned and greeted us with a smile.

"Hey, man," Adam said. He was the kind of guy who was all personality and charm, and I could see why Vaughn liked him. He gave a great first impression. "I was wondering what happened to you guys. We got separated at the light and I never saw y'all again. Did you finish the ride?" He looked around as if searching for Vaughn. "Where's Vaughn? Does he need a ride back home? He's on my way so it's no trouble."

"He had a mishap over by the park," Jack said. "He blew a tire and bent a rim and went down pretty hard."

"No way!" Adam said. "Man, that sucks. That bike is brand new. I bet he's ticked."

"That's an understatement," Jack said. "But he'll be fine and the bike will get fixed. It happens."

"Yeah," Adam said. "I hit a rock once going forty-five on a downhill and went ass over elbow into the ditch. I woke up two days later in the hospital. Rattled my brains pretty good."

"Do you mind if we talk to you for a couple of minutes?" Jack asked. "It's about Brett Jorgenson."

"Oh, yeah," Adam said, nodding. "Sure. It's terrible what happened to him. It really makes you think about how vulnerable we are out there. All it takes is a guy driving by and not paying attention and then it's all over in a flash. But at least he turned himself in. It doesn't bring Brett back, but it at least gives his poor wife some closure. I can't imagine what she's going through right now."

"I completed the autopsy yesterday and discovered something interesting," I said.

Adam looked at me quizzically.

"Brett wasn't killed because of the hit-and-run," I said. "Brett was murdered. Someone spiked his water bottles with amphetamines and his heart exploded."

Adam's face showed confusion, immediately followed by shock. He seemed genuinely surprised by the news.

"How's that even possible?" Adam asked. "No one would want to kill Brett."

"That's what we're trying to find out," Jack said. "You see, someone would've had to switch his water bottles after the ride Thursday night. Brett had a routine. He'd prep his bike immediately for his ride the next morning. It wouldn't be hard to switch his bottles with the spiked ones. He'd never know the difference."

Adam's eyes went even wider. "That means you think it was someone in Old Dominion who killed Brett?" He shook his head and put his hands on his hips. "No way. Not possible. I know all those guys. No one would do anything like that."

"Except it's true and Brett is dead," Jack said. "But maybe Brett wasn't the intended target."

"What do you mean?" he asked.

"Can you explain how we found your fingerprints on Brett's water bottles?" Jack asked. "The same water bottles that came back with positive traces of amphetamines?"

"Wait, what?" Adam said. "You've got to be joking."

"I try to make it a point not to joke about murder," Jack said. "You take Adderall, don't you?"

Adam looked confused for a moment and asked, "What does that have to do with anything? I used to take it, but I'm in a trial program with the military and I haven't taken any in almost a month. I don't understand."

"Adderall is an amphetamine," I said. "It doesn't take much to overdose. It gets the heart pumping. Shortness of breath. Hallucinations. Confusion.

Panic. All things Brett Jorgenson probably experienced before he died. On someone with a normal, healthy heart, it might not kill them. But Brett didn't have a normal healthy heart. But the killer wouldn't know that."

Adam paled and licked his lips. "This is crazy. I liked Brett. I would never do something like that to him. There has to be an explanation."

Jack moved in a little closer, his size intimidating. But Adam didn't budge an inch. He was probably used to people being in his face after years in the military. If anything, he stood up straighter and faced Jack head-on.

"This doesn't look good for you," Jack told him softly. "We've got your fingerprints on Brett's water bottles and your drugs as the murder weapon of choice. But I think you're right about liking Brett. About it being a mistake. Because Brett wasn't your target. It was Vaughn."

"Vaughn?" Adam asked, color flooding into his cheeks. "Why the hell would I try and kill Vaughn? This doesn't make any sense."

"I don't think you tried to kill him," Jack said. "You just wanted to throw him off course. Someone has been working overtime to make sure the people closest to me are out of commission recently. Because when the people closest to me are hurt, my focus isn't on the job, the election, or the fact that

AvantGuard is trying to take over my county and do whatever the hell the want to do. They're trying to buy and intimidate an elected office. So how do you fit into all of this?"

"I really have no idea what you're talking about," Adam said. "I don't know anything about an election. Vaughn is my friend."

"Is that all he is?" Jack asked. "Maybe you thought it would be easiest to get close to him if he thought you were gay. You hang out a few times. Give him rides. Have access to his bike and water bottles.

"Maybe you've been off the Adderall for a few weeks, but I bet you still have a prescription bottle full of pills lying around somewhere just in case. Though I'm guessing the pill bottle isn't so full now. Everyone has the same water bottles, so you spike the water, add in some electrolyte powder to disguise the taste, and slip them into the cages when no one is looking. Only you weren't planning on Vaughn's new bike. It'd be easy to get them mixed up when everyone's bikes are scattered after a ride and put them in Brett's cages by mistake. It was an accident, right Adam?"

Adam seemed to snap out of it at the sound of his name. His face had lost all color and there was a sheen of sweat on his brow.

"I was in the military," Jack said. "I know how things work. You bust your ass to follow orders and be a good soldier and move up the ranks. But there's always someone ahead of you. And then you start to rise up and you realize it's politics, just like everything else. It's who can do for who instead of who's the most qualified or deserving. What did they promise you? Money? Rank? A job? You kind of blew your cover when you and Leslie were feeling each other up a few minutes ago."

"Wait a second," Adam said, putting up his hands and scrubbing the sides of his face. "This is nuts. I don't know what you're talking about. I didn't kill Brett. And I'm bi. That's no secret. Leslie and I have had a thing a time or two. I've hooked up with several people in the group. That's what everyone does. It's no secret.

"And Vaughn is perfectly aware that I'm the way I am. I don't want a serious relationship, and he doesn't want to play the field. I'm cool with that. So we're friends. I didn't kill Brett, and I don't know anything about amphetamines."

"How'd your prints get on the water bottles?" Jack asked.

Adam started to shake his head and open his mouth, but he froze before he could speak. He closed his eyes and shook his head, as if he were trying to make sense of it all.

"What is it?" Jack asked.

"I don't know," he said, tapping his hand against his

thigh. I'd noticed he'd become more jittery the longer we'd talked. "I...I don't feel so good. I need to go."

"I hope you're going to get an attorney," Jack said. "Because it looks like you're going to need one. We'll be in touch."

We moved out of the way as Adam got into his Jeep and threw it into reverse. He fishtailed out of the parking lot and sped away.

"I wonder what that's all about," I said.

"I don't know," Jack said. "We'll let him stew on it, and then bring him in for formal questioning tomorrow. He seems a little nervous."

"I'm guessing he's not going to do too well in the trial he's taking part in to do away with his meds."

"I hope he's got some left," Jack said. "Let's go back home and see what else Carver has pieced together. And maybe you can figure out a way to explain to Vaughn that we think his friend is a murderer."

"The fun never ends with this job," I said.

17

SOMETHING ABOUT ADAM TAYLOR BOTHERED ME, but I couldn't put my finger on it.

I was hoping to avoid Vaughn and Jack's mother when we got back to the house, but they were still in the kitchen with notebooks and charts and graphs spread across all the counters. I froze in the entryway and Jack looked back at me when I didn't follow him toward the chaos.

"What's wrong?" he asked.

"I don't know," I said. "I kind of want snacks, but I don't want to get caught up in whatever they're doing in there for the next five hours. I want to go fill in the murder board and get some work done."

Jack pursed his lips and said, "This is one of those 'for better or worse' moments, right? Go ahead and start with the board and give Carver a call. I'll secure the snacks and hopefully get them to you sometime in the near future. If you don't hear from me in twenty minutes, I'd go ahead and order a pizza."

"Sounds like a plan," I said, kissing him quickly on the cheek and running down the hall to his office before he could change his mind.

It wasn't that I didn't want to hang out with Vaughn and Mrs. Lawson, but I was an introvert by nature and I needed a break from people for a little while. I checked the time and decided to call into the funeral home and make sure everything was set for the viewing, but when I walked into the office and saw Brett's picture on the wall along with fourteen people he called friends, I lost my train of thought and went to stand in front of it.

The spider's web was more entangled than it had been the day before. Relationships made everything more complicated, and sexual relationships even more so. Adam Taylor was a military guy. He was used to taking orders. The question was, who was giving him the orders?

I turned on the laptop and downloaded the finger-print match Morgenstern had pulled from the bottle and a copy of the Adderall prescription Carver had sent over. If Adam got an attorney worth his salt, he was going to want to know how we found out about the Adderall from a sealed military file.

Then there was the relationship between Adam and Leslie. And then Ginny and Benji. Ginny had lived in King George her whole life, and she was a doctor. She'd certainly know about amphetamines, but I couldn't see how or why she'd want Adam to target Vaughn. She had no connections to Vaughn personally that I could see. No connections to Brett either for that matter, other than failing at adding him as a notch on her bedpost.

Carver had sent a lot of financial information, and I threw it all on the screen with the corresponding parties just because, but it only confused things, and Carver was right. Everyone in that bike club was doing more than okay in the financial department.

Jack came in a few minutes later, and I realized he'd barely overshot the twenty-minute mark. But he came in with a charcuterie board and a pitcher of tea, so I could forgive his tardiness.

"My mom sends her regards," he said, holding up the food. "She said this is for you and I can only have some if you feel like sharing. Which you do."

"I don't know," I said, smiling. "I'm an only child. I'm not really good with sharing. And your mom said she likes me best anyway. What are you going to give me if I share?" I moved in closer and put my fingers lightly on the waistband of his jeans.

"That's a loaded question if I've ever heard one," he said. "You know what the penalty is for bribing a peace officer?"

"I hope it's life," I said, moving in to kiss him. And then I snatched the board out of his hands and stuck a cube of cheese in my mouth. "I love you. Please have some charcuterie."

He exhaled loudly and adjusted his jeans and said, "You drive me crazy."

"That's good, right?" I asked. "Think how bored you'd be if I didn't. You drive me crazy too. That's what makes this good."

Jack grunted and looked at the work I'd done on the board. "Who's giving the orders?" he asked, echoing my sentiment.

"He's military," I said. And then we both looked at each other.

"AvantGuard," Jack said.

"You think this is about the privatized prisons?" I asked.

"I think this is about making sure I lose the election," Jack said. "AvantGuard is a private security company, but it's militarized and most of their employees are former military with special skills. Maybe Adam has special skills we don't know about.

"There's no way we can get anything out of Avant-Guard. You can't even walk in the front door without being fingerprinted and a background check run. If Carver really managed to get into their system, first of all, that's probably the most impressive thing he's ever done. And second of all, I'd have no idea where to start looking and how we could connect the dots."

"Might as well call him," I said. "I need to check in with the funeral home anyway."

Jack grunted and took out his cell phone and I did the same. It took several rings before Emmy Lu picked up the phone.

"Sorry about that," she said. "Things have been busy."

"With the viewing?" I asked. "I know there was a lot of out-of-town family coming in."

"No, with the reporters," she said. "They're camped out front again. Plus a man came by and asked if the funeral home was for sale and how he'd like to make you an offer you can't refuse. I very politely told him to take a hike. And the grave-digging crew never showed up at the cemetery, but I called my dad and he got a couple of his friends together and they're over at the graveyard taking care of it now. We'll be all good for the burial tomorrow. Oh, and Lucinda Marks' daughter called. She passed away a few minutes ago and Sheldon took the Suburban to go retrieve her from the hospital. We'll put her in the cooler until you can come in for the autopsy."

I looked at my watch and said, "I'll either do it late tonight after everyone clears out or in the morning. They bought a burial plan so everything is ready to go."

"Now we just have to keep our fingers crossed that nothing else goes wrong or someone doesn't accidentally open a fire hydrant on those reporters. My brother is a firefighter, you know. It'd be worth it to see them washing away down the street."

"Just a few more days and they'll be gone," I said. "And I'm giving the staff the whole week of Thanksgiving paid vacation time. You guys have earned it."

"I would've settled for the free booze at the victory party Tuesday night. I'm a cheap date. Gotta go."

She hung up so fast I wondered what else had happened, but I knew whatever it was, they could handle it. The funeral home was in good hands.

"Everything okay?" Jack asked.

"Same old, same old," I said. "And someone came by to make an offer on the funeral home."

"You never know," Jack said, "If we lose Tuesday maybe we could sell everything and buy a motorhome and travel around the country."

"Yeah, you'd love that for about seventy-two hours," I said.

"Is this one of those conversations where I should wait until you're finished?" Carver asked.

"Hey, Carver," I said. "I didn't know you were on the line."

"It's okay," he said. "Magnolia and I are always fascinated by your conversations. Don't let us interrupt you."

"Things are working out between you and Magnolia, huh?" I asked, giving Jack a teasing wink. "I think this is the longest you've been with one woman."

"Hush, lady," Carver said. "Are you trying to get me killed? Magnolia will kill me in my sleep."

I looked at Jack and whispered, "He does know Magnolia is a computer, right?"

"I heard that," Carver said. "Fortunately, I covered Magnolia's ears, so she didn't hear your treachery."

"Computers have ears?" I mouthed to Jack and he shrugged.

"So here's what we know," Jack said. "We don't have any reason to believe that Brett Jorgenson was the intended target. We can't find motive. But we can find motive if Vaughn becomes the target. He has the same bike as Brett, same water bottles, and the stem was cut on his tire before his ride today.

The pressure built up and caused him to have a blowout."

I looked at Jack with raised eyebrows since this was the first I was hearing of this information.

"I took a detour while my mom was making snacks," Jack said. "That's why I was a few minutes late."

"You guys have snacks?" Carver asked. "I love snacks."

"You love anything you can put into your mouth," Jack said.

"Which is why Michelle and I are coming to your victory party Tuesday night. Free food and drinks. Can't beat that. And it's a bonus if you win."

"Thank you," Jack said dryly. "Anyway, I thought the tire would be blown past the point of recognition, but there was a small cut in the rubber, just above where the stem was where you'd air the tire up. It was made by a sharp blade. There were no jagged edges or tears, so I know it didn't occur after the blowout. A cut like that would make the pressure build up as you rode until it exploded."

"Someone sabotaged my bike?" Vaughn asked from the doorway.

Jack and I froze and then turned to see Vaughn and Jeri staring at us with equal expressions of horror.

18

"WE DIDN'T MEAN TO PRY," JERI SAID. "BUT I WAS going to see if you wanted more to eat, and Vaughn needed to ask a question about an ad airing tomorrow."

"Y'all might as well come in and hear all of it then," Jack said. "But nothing leaves this room until we have someone behind bars."

Jeri pretended like she was zipping her lips and stepped into the room, and Vaughn followed behind her more hesitantly.

"Is that Mrs. Lawson?" Carver asked.

"Benjamin," Jeri said, clapping her hands together. "It's so good to hear your voice. You're doing well? I missed you when you were in town. *Someone* didn't tell me you were here until you'd already left."

"Don't worry," Carver said. "You can fawn over me when we come to the victory party on Tuesday. I keep telling my wife that you're the one that sets the bar on how to treat a man. Maybe you could give her some tips."

Jeri's grin lit up her face. "Darling, the fact she hasn't killed you yet is a miracle. It sounds like she's doing just fine to me."

"Figures," Carver said. "A man in a wheelchair can't catch a break."

"I don't mean to interrupt," Vaughn said. "But could someone tell me what the hell is going on?" He was standing in front of the whiteboard and the familiar faces displayed there.

Jack blew out a breath. "You might need to sit down for this."

"I think you might be right," Vaughn said and moved to one of the chairs around the conference table.

Jack filled them in on Brett Jorgenson's murder, Floyd muddying the works with the hit-and-run, and the drugs found in Brett's tox screen.

"So what's the deal?" Vaughn asked. "I heard you say I was the target. What does that mean?"

"Honestly," Jack said. "I think everyone in this room is the target. I think as we keep peeling back layers, we're going to find that AvantGuard is undermining the election in any way they can. They're throwing money at it. They're bribing who they need to bribe. And if that doesn't work to sway the election, they're trying to divert my attention. The best way to do that is to cause chaos in my life and in the lives of the people I love. By leaking information to Floyd for a newspaper article. Or getting my mom kicked out of the country club."

"Or trying to kill me," Vaughn said matter-of-factly.

"Yes," Jack said. "Though I'm not convinced they wanted to kill you. Brett had a history of cocaine use that had weakened his heart, so the amphetamines worked him over pretty good. You probably would've just passed out while you were riding."

"And the tire today?" he asked.

"Same thing," Jack said. "Take you out of the election game for a little while. You're in charge of the money."

"AvantGuard," Vaughn said, narrowing his eyes. "I knew that sounded familiar. They sent a rep out to me months ago. Maybe a year. They wanted to donate a hefty amount to your campaign in exchange for support for the prison contract."

"How much money?" Jack asked.

"Twenty million dollars," Vaughn said.

"They wanted to throw twenty mil at a local sheriff's election?" I asked dumbfounded.

Vaughn shrugged. "It happens all the time, especially with the spread of social media and the news in our faces all the time. It's not uncommon for big out-of-state donors to throw money at smaller elections in different states just to stack the deck the way they want it."

"Well, it's stupid," I said. "Everyone should worry about their own state and mind their own business. Those guys at AvantGuard don't know what it's like to be a regular citizen here. What farm life is like or the needs of the people in a rural community. I can't believe they'd try and throw that much money away."

"A government contract for privatized prisons would bring them ten times that amount and then doubled again," Jack said. "It's a never-ending cash cow, and there are a lot of people who are angry we've thwarted their plans."

"They were very persuasive," Vaughn said. "But I never even entertained the idea or thought of bringing it to you. I knew how you felt, and anyone with half a brain can see what it would do to us."

"Progress paves the way to hell," Jeri said, making everyone laugh.

"So why is Adam's picture highlighted on your board?" Vaughn asked.

"Because his fingerprints were found on Brett Jorgenson's water bottles," I said gently. "And he has a prescription for Adderall, which is more than likely the lethal dosage of amphetamine found in Brett's system."

"So you think it was Adam that was trying to do that to me?" he asked, shaking his head. "I can't see it." He held up his hand. "And don't say I'm naïve or that I don't want to see it. I read people well. It comes with the territory. Adam is reckless and selfish and he likes to play fast and hard. He likes to take things to the extreme, whether it's his relationships or his athletic activities. His poker face is about as good as J.J's. He wouldn't be able to cover it up if his purpose was to take me down."

"I think I resent that," I said. "My poker face is much better than it used to be."

"Mmm," Jeri said, shaking her head. "We all have our strengths, dear."

"How do you explain the fingerprints and the drugs?" Jack asked.

"I don't know," Vaughn said. "Any one of those people could have access to the drugs. Hell, several of them are doctors and one is a former addict. Everyone else is rich enough to buy whatever they want. As far as fingerprints, I just don't see Adam knowingly putting poisoned bottles in Brett's cages. Or my cages for that matter."

"You think someone else told him to do it?" I asked.

"It's very possible," Vaughn said. "You've seen the rides. It's total chaos and movement. How hard would it be for someone to walk up and say, 'Hey, these are Vaughn's. Go put them on his bike.'?"

Jack nodded. "Only Brett's bike looks just like yours."

"Yeah," Vaughn said. "Just like mine."

I could see the guilt on his face, and I knew he was thinking if he'd only gotten a different bike, a different color…or something. Then maybe Brett would still be alive.

"What about Adam's relationship with Leslie Carron?" Jack asked. "When we questioned him this morning he said you weren't interested in each other romantically."

"Oh, he's interested," Vaughn said. "But Adam is still in the screw-anything-that-moves phase. I have no desire to be on the sexual merry-go-round. I want to settle down, have a family. And that's the last thing he wants."

"Ginny Grant?" Jack asked.

Vaughn scoffed. "Women, men…It makes no difference to Adam as long as you want to have fun. Ginny is basically the female version of Adam, so they tend to circle back around to each other."

"Who else does he play with?" I asked.

"In our current group? Vaughn asked. "All the single women except Zoe Krantz. She's a ballbuster. He and Leslie dated a few months exclusively, but I think she did it to make Benji jealous. And he had a brief fling with Gloria Padgett that everyone knows about but Mitch."

"Oh, he knows," Jack's mother said. "Your father was the one who told me about it. He said it was making the rounds on the golf course one day."

"Huh," Vaughn said. "Interesting."

"And there's no tension between Adam and Mitch?" I asked.

"Not that I can tell," Vaughn said. "Business as usual."

"What about the men?" Jack asked.

Vaughn blew out a breath. "Most of the club is strictly hetero, but Adam got Benji to swing as long as Leslie was in the mix. Benji is obsessed with Leslie. He'd lie naked on broken glass if she told him to."

Jack's mother had gotten up from her seat and moved to the board so she could see it better and then she gasped. "You're talking about Leslie Carron?" she asked.

"Yeah, you know her?" Vaughn asked.

"She's the one! She's the one who complained about me to the board and got us kicked out." Jeri's face was scarlet with rage. "She acts all prim and proper like she's the Queen of England in her uptight suits, and then she makes passive-aggressive statements on how we could change things or do them better. And then she'll donate money and we'll get a memo announcing the changes she suggested. Maybe she's sleeping with everyone. I wouldn't be surprised at all if she voted for Floyd. Trash recognizes trash in my opinion."

My lips twitched, and I covered my mouth with my hand so she wouldn't see my smile and think I was making fun of her.

"If I could cut in," Carver said. "Magnolia and I were just getting to the good stuff when the two of you walked in. It's funny you should mention this love triangle because Leslie Carron is the project manager for Watermark Real Estate Developers. Which probably means nothing to you, except that Watermark is one of the companies I told you about yesterday who is buying up land in King George. And Watermark is owned by Trident."

"And Trident is owned by AvantGuard," Jack said.

"Bingo," Carver said. "This woman makes a nice mid-six figures a year plus bonuses. And she was a marine. I told you two of your suspects were military. As soon as AvantGaurd started popping up those were the two I focused on. She's skilled in hand-to-hand and an expert marksman. And she'll sell you oceanfront property while she slits your throat."

"Doesn't this bother you?" Vaughn asked Jack. "Don't you see what this is? There is someone out there who hates you so much that he's willing to make sure that not only you fail, but everyone you love fails too. This person is willing to burn King George to the ground to get to you."

Jack put his hands in his pockets and leaned against his desk. "I guess when you put it that way. But I don't know if it has to do with me personally, or just that I'm in the way of what they want to accomplish."

"Either way," Vaughn said. "It sucks. And these people need to be stopped."

"All I can do is work within the law on my level," Jack said. "And my level is figuring out who killed Brett Jorgenson. All of this other stuff in the periphery," he said, waving his hand. "There's no crime. Just inconvenience."

"Which is why you have federal friends in very high places," Carver said. "There are some very questionable dealings happening at AvantGuard that I think the FBI will be interested in."

As they were talking the pieces of the puzzle started to click together. "Adam really didn't know what we were talking about this morning when we confronted him," I said. "But when you asked him how the bottles got into Brett's cages something clicked. He knew it was Leslie. She'd have given him the bottles and he'd have thought nothing of it. And she'd have known about his Adderall prescription and was probably able to take what she needed without him noticing since he wasn't taking them."

I looked at Jack with urgency. "He knows. He knew it had to be her. That's why he was acting so weird. He was going to confront her."

"Let's go," Jack said, tossing me my phone. "Maybe we can get there in time to save Adam Taylor from being taken away in a body bag."

I didn't hold out much hope.

19

Jack got on the radio as soon as we got into the Tahoe and put out an APB for Adam Taylor's Jeep and Leslie Carron's Lexus. And then he had units dispatched to both Adam's and Leslie's homes.

As soon as we hit open road he hit the lights and sirens.

"Adam was just an easy target for her," I said. "She played the game Adam wanted her to play, and she saw an opening to use him. She works for a company who always gets what they want. She'll kill him if she can get away with it."

"I know," Jack said, pressing harder on the accelerator.

The call came back on the radio that Adam's Jeep had been spotted in his driveway, but no one was answering the door and when they'd entered the premises there was no sign of anyone except his cat.

"Where would they go?" I asked.

"The bike," Jack said and then asked into the radio, "Is there a bike on the rack of the Jeep or in his garage?"

There was silence for a few seconds before a response came back. "Negative," the officer replied. "There's no sign of a bicycle."

"She took his bike?" I asked.

"Easiest and cleanest way to get rid of Adam is to make it look like an accident. She comes to meet him. He confronts her. And she somehow incapacitates him, maybe a blow to the back of the head."

"He's a big guy with military training," I said.

"And her training makes his look like toddlers playing in a sandbox. She could take him down, dump him in her trunk, and then take his bike and rack it on her car." Jack put on the brakes and did a U-turn in the middle of the road. "Then she'd take him somewhere along their regular route. But not too populated an area. She wouldn't want anyone to find him right away."

"Sheriff," a woman's voice called out.

Barbara Blanton's voice could be recognized underwater it was so distinctive. She had a high nasal voice with a Southern drawl I'd never been completely convinced was genuine. But no matter how she talked, listening to her was like nails on a chalkboard.

"I'm here," Jack said.

"I just got a call from Florence Babbins on my cell," Barbara said. "She's got a police scanner so she heard the APB go out. She likes to listen for entertainment."

"What'd she say?" Jack said, gritting his teeth with impatience.

"She said she saw a black Lexus fitting the APB description turn onto Route 11 about five minutes ago. It caught her eye because a water bottle fell off the bike on the back of the car and into the street."

"God bless Florence Babbins," Jack said. "Call Vaughn and put it on speaker."

I did as he asked and Vaughn answered on the first ring.

"Do you have your group routes saved in your phone?" Jack asked.

"Sure," Vaughn said. "What do you need?"

"Is there a ride that takes you on Route 11?"

"I'll send it to your phone," he said. "Anything else?"

"Where's the most desolate stretch of that ride?"

"Actually, that ride will take you along County Road 36."

"Thanks," Jack said softly and I hung up the phone. And then he slammed his fist against the steering wheel.

"We're not far from 36," I told him.

"I know," he said. "I just don't have a good feeling about what we're going to find when we get there."

Jack turned off his lights and sirens and then called in the route so units could come in from all directions in case we somehow missed her.

"Will catching Leslie help Carver start an FBI investigation on AvantGuard?" I asked.

"Nope," Jack said. "By the time we're done here Leslie Carron won't have a file at all. I doubt that's even her real name anyway. Those private contractors like to pretend they're a law unto themselves. They're deadly and dangerous, and Leslie is one of their own. She's a pawn, just like Adam was to her. But even the lower-level pawns are nobody to mess with. If Carver opens a bag of worms into Avant-Guard, then I hope he's prepared for the fight of his life because what he's been through with the wreck and the surgeries is nothing."

"Sometimes I wish we were like all the regular people out there," I said. "Living in complete ignorance of all the horrible things that could happen in an instant."

"Open the glove box," Jack said. "There's a weapon and an extra magazine, just in case."

My fingers flexed automatically and I opened the glove box. After I'd almost been strangled by a serial killer, I'd carried a gun religiously. It went everywhere with me—from the shower to the grocery store. But after Jack and I had gotten married I'd carried it less and less, until time went by and I realized I hadn't been carrying it at all.

My hand wrapped around the butt of the pistol and I put it in my lap.

The radio was nonstop as units gave their positions. Cole was coming from the opposite direction so we'd meet up somewhere on 36. It would take Leslie time to remove Adam's body from the trunk and stage him. I wasn't sure how she planned on killing him, but there were only so many ways she could do it that wouldn't scream *murder* as soon as I got him on my table.

The dangerous thing about County Road 36 was that the hills were so steep it was impossible to see a car until you were cresting over a hill and down into the valley. Jack slowed his speed some, but there wasn't much he could do but go forward and hope that we found Leslie's black Lexus before she disposed of Adam.

I was starting to think we might be on the wrong road altogether when I saw the afternoon sun glint off metal. The black Lexus was parked at the bottom of the hill on the side of the road and the bike rack was empty, but the car was running.

Jack sped up and I searched the steep ditch for any sign of movement.

"There," I said, seeing the bike first and then the body next to it. But not Leslie. "I don't see her."

Jack flipped his lights back on and parked the Tahoe haphazardly so it would be hard for her to get her car around it, and then he said, "Stay in the car."

This was the part of the job I hated. Not for myself, but for Jack. It was one thing to know the person you loved most in the world was putting on a uniform and placing himself in danger on a daily basis. But it was another thing entirely to see it firsthand.

Jack got out of the Tahoe and had his weapon in his hand so fast I barely saw him reach for it.

"Leslie Carron," Jack called out. "This is Sheriff Lawson. We need to ask you a few questions."

Jack looked inside her vehicle to make sure there was no one inside and he reached in the open car window and turned off the ignition. I gripped the pistol tightly and it felt familiar and right in my hand. I watched as he moved around the back of the car and toward the ditch.

I never saw which direction she came from. A black blur barreled toward Jack and slammed into the center of his body, and then I heard his gun hit the pavement as she did something to his wrist to disarm him. But Jack had been ready for her and came up with a punch under her chin that had her reeling backward.

I'd not seen Jack fight hand to hand, not since we were kids, but clearly he'd had training somewhere along the way and I thanked God for it. Because Leslie Carron was good. Very good. It was hard to fight with that level of power and intensity for long, but they were fighting for survival.

I got on the radio and told Cole to hurry, but I wasn't sure anyone heard me because my voice went hoarse as I saw her pull a knife from her boot and swipe across Jack's middle. He arched his body and dodged out of the way, but I could see the slice across his shirt.

Way too close.

It was easy to see now why she made it a point to blend in and do what others were doing. Her entire body was a weapon. The knife was an extension in her hand as she sliced and Jack blocked. They were both breathing heavily and I knew at some point something would have to give. Only one would walk away.

I didn't hear sirens and I didn't know how far away the other units were. All I knew was that I wasn't going to watch my husband die. I knew how to handle a weapon, and I wasn't going to sit in the car like a wilting flower while Samurai Barbie sliced Jack to pieces.

I opened the car door, planning to take cover on the opposite side of it, but I barely had my feet on solid ground before she pivoted and flung the knife in my direction. It happened so quickly I wasn't sure what had happened. There'd been no sting. Adrenaline had acted as a painkiller. But when I looked down I saw the flesh of my arm pinned to the car door.

Without the knife in her hand Jack moved in quickly. He was bigger and stronger and she was no match for dirty street fighting. He bulldozed her and picked her up around the waist, tossing her to the ground, but her feet came up and hit his chest as he moved to follow her down and pin her.

I couldn't take a shot. Not without risking Jack. But if he went down I was ready to shoot every bullet I had. And then I heard the sweet sound of sirens in the distance. The hills and valleys made the echo chamber seem like they were farther away than they were because in moments they were cresting the hill and coming toward us.

The sound of help on the way must have invigorated Jack because he countered with a blow that knocked her off her feet. It was all he needed to get a knee in her back and get her subdued.

Cops were swarming from all directions, and Cole stopped to check on me as he passed by, noting the knife in my arm.

"I'm fine," I said. "Go help him."

My voice trembled as much as my hands, and I watched as Leslie Carron was cuffed and Jack was able to stand up. He was a mess. His clothes were sliced and torn and blood soaked his shirt and around his collar. His lip was split and bleeding and he was going to have some interesting bruises. But he was alive.

He walked toward me, his eyes on the knife and his mouth getting thinner the closer he got. He stopped a foot away from me and said, "I told you to stay in the car."

"Yeah," I said. "But I'm not going to apologize. You wouldn't have sat in the car if you'd been watching me getting beaten to a bloody pulp. And look on the bright side, I got the knife out of her hand. Your shirt looks like it was designed by Edward Scissorhands. You're a mess."

"You're not doing so hot yourself," he said, studying my arm and then the area behind it where the knife had embedded into the door. "It's not too bad. You'll have a nice scar."

"Just what I always wanted," I said, starting to worry when he tore off part of his tattered shirt. "Wait a sec —" But I didn't get to finish the sentence before he had the knife pulled out and the cloth pressed against the wound.

"You did that as payback," I said, sucking in a deep breath and letting it out slowly.

"Yep," he said, and then he leaned down to kiss me. "Adam Taylor is still alive. He's unconscious, but alive. We made it in time."

"That's something then," I said. "Is it bad that I was hoping it was Floyd behind all of this? I'd really like to put him in jail. Or shoot him with a Taser."

Jack chuckled. "Don't worry about Floyd. People like him always get their due. What do you say we make a quick stop for stitches and then spend the rest of the evening letting my mother fuss over us?"

"I like that idea," I said, getting back into the car.

"I'm glad," he said. "Because I have a feeling that once I lie down, it might be a while before I can get up again."

"You fought good," I told him. "Try not to make a habit of it."

He laughed and then groaned as he got into the Tahoe to drive us to the hospital. I couldn't think of a better happily-ever-after. We were alive and whole. At least for now. Whatever was brewing in King George County was bigger than the two of us or the police department. Uncertainty was like a black cloud hanging over us, but we'd never turned our backs on a fight, and we'd never stopped working for those who no longer had a voice. I just prayed we weren't collecting casualties while we were fighting a battle we might not ever win.

EPILOGUE

THIS LIFE WAS STILL NEW TO ME.

I'd spent most of my life trying to hide from the public eye, trying to avoid gossip and probing questions. I'd learned to keep things close to the vest and that there were very few people in this world you could count on or trust.

That had been the old me who'd lived in the shadows of her parents and the life they'd chosen to live. But marriage to Jack hadn't given me a choice on whether or not I wanted to stay in the shadows. And it made me realize that I didn't belong there. That I had family and friends, none of which were mine by blood, but who all belonged to me by heart.

I wasn't an emotional person for the most part, but standing next to Jack and looking out over a crowd of familiar, smiling faces made my chest tight. This was our community—the people who supported us no matter what was splashed in the news or gossipers said. These were the people who supported us and wanted us to succeed. And I was realizing having those kinds of people in your life was not only important, but also necessary. Seeing the good in humanity made me want to learn to be a better friend.

I smoothed my gown nervously and straightened my shoulders. This was Jack's night, and if he'd wanted me to show up in a circus tent, I would've done it. But the victory party was a formal event, and Jack had donned his tuxedo and managed to look like a Hollywood A-lister instead of a small county sheriff. The shadowed bruises along his jaw and around his mouth only added an aura of mystique. And if he was moving a little stiff, I figured I was the only one to notice.

I was always self-conscious next to Jack. He exuded life and vitality, and he was beautiful to look at all the time, and there were many times I wondered how or why he'd picked me. It was amazing how the self-consciousness that plagued me in my youth had followed me into adulthood. But Jack made me feel beautiful, even if I didn't consider myself as such.

Fortunately, Jack's mother had come through for me with a long, strapless column of black silk that fit like a glove and shoes that were going to make my feet have regrets for the next few days. I wore a black cloth around my bicep to cover my stitches, but no one could tell it didn't belong there.

I felt proud to stand next to Jack—the doubt about my worth and position and appearance faded to the background—and for the first time I felt like I belonged.

It wouldn't matter if Jack won or lost the election. Those things in life that relied on human nature were fleeting. But Jack and I were solid, and we always would be. And no matter what happened regarding his son, we would deal with it together.

I grabbed Jack's hand and squeezed it as I scanned the sea of faces that filled the tent behind Lombardi's. My stomach was a knot and the champagne glass in my hand was nothing more than a prop as we waited for the final results of the election to come in.

"Relax," Jack leaned down and whispered into my ear.

"Easy for you to say." I tried to smile and straightened his bow tie. "My whole status depends on the outcome of this election. How am I supposed to get out of parking tickets if you can't fix them for me?"

"I knew there had to be a reason you married me," he said, pulling me closer.

"There was a very good reason. Why don't we ditch this joint and I'll show you why?"

"Give me ten minutes and I'm all yours," Jack said. "I think someone wants to talk to us."

I pouted and turned to see who was interrupting, and I squeezed Jack's hand harder when I saw Charles Wilson making his way toward us. Charlie was the clerk of courts and would be the first to have official election results.

"Sheriff," he said, shaking Jack's hand and clapping him on the back.

I'd noticed the people around us had stopped talking to see what was happening.

"How do you feel about four more years?" Charlie asked.

I felt the relief in Jack even as the crowd around us exploded into cheers. It was a good night to celebrate with good people. There would be other times to worry about the job or the next election, but tonight wasn't that night.

"Four more years sounds good," Jack said, grinning. "Really good."

"You won by a landslide," Charlie said. "King George loves you and your whole family." He leaned in a little closer. "My wife and I returned our country club membership. Between you and me and the fence post, I've heard more than thirty people have resigned because of what they did to your parents. People will learn we don't like outsiders coming in and ruining a good thing."

"I don't think you have anything to worry about," Jack said. "I believe we made our point to those guys at AvantGuard. They're going to have to find someplace else to stage a takeover."

"Good for you, son," Charlie said. "But be careful. Those guys don't mind playing dirty, and if you don't mind me saying, and the hand they had in this election, I think you've got a mighty powerful enemy over there."

Jack nodded soberly. "You don't see the things I've seen and not have enemies. It's learning how to recognize them that's the hard part. But I'll be ready."

"I'm sure you will," Charlie said. "We've got faith in you. In both of you." Charlie looked at me with a twinkle in his eyes. "Now I believe you have a victory speech to make."

Charlie disappeared in the crowd and Jack pulled me into his arms and kissed me. "I promise to make it a very short speech. Five minutes, tops. And then we can continue where we left off."

"Congratulations, Sheriff," I said. "No one deserves this more than you. I'm proud of you."

"Two minutes," he said, winking at me and making his way onstage to cheers.

There would always be crime, and there would always be death. But for this moment, life was perfect.

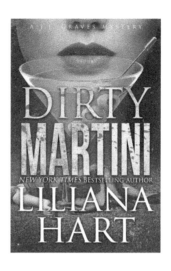

The next installment of the New York Times best-selling series by Liliana Hart...

When a friend from medical school shows up on J.J. Graves' doorstep in distress, J.J. offers her a sanctuary. But the woman has brought trouble to Bloody Mary, and no one is safe.

Coming May 11, 2021! Pre-order Today

ABOUT THE AUTHOR

Liliana Hart is a *New York Times*, *USA Today*, and Publisher's Weekly bestselling author of more than sixty titles. After starting her first novel her freshman year of college, she immediately became addicted to writing and knew she'd found what she was meant to do with her life. She has no idea why she majored in music.

Since publishing in June 2011, Liliana has sold more than six-million books. All three of her series have made multiple appearances on the *New York Times* list.

Liliana can almost always be found at her computer writing, hauling five kids to various activities, or spending time with her husband. She calls Texas home.

If you enjoyed reading this, I would appreciate it if you would help others enjoy this book, too.

Recommend it. Please help other readers find this book by recommending it to friends, readers' groups and discussion boards.

Review it. Please tell other readers why you liked this book by reviewing.

Connect with me online:
www.lilianahart.com

facebook.com/LilianaHart

instagram.com/LilianaHart

bookbub.com/authors/liliana-hart

ALSO BY LILIANA HART

JJ Graves Mystery Series

Dirty Little Secrets

A Dirty Shame

Dirty Rotten Scoundrel

Down and Dirty

Dirty Deeds

Dirty Laundry

Dirty Money

A Dirty Job

Dirty Devil

Playing Dirty

Dirty Martini

Addison Holmes Mystery Series

Whiskey Rebellion

Whiskey Sour

Whiskey For Breakfast

Whiskey, You're The Devil

Whiskey on the Rocks

Whiskey Tango Foxtrot

Whiskey and Gunpowder

Whiskey Lullaby

The Scarlet Chronicles

Bouncing Betty

Hand Grenade Helen

Front Line Francis

The Harley and Davidson Mystery Series

The Farmer's Slaughter

A Tisket a Casket

I Saw Mommy Killing Santa Claus

Get Your Murder Running

Deceased and Desist

Malice in Wonderland

Tequila Mockingbird

Gone With the Sin

Grime and Punishment

Blazing Rattles

A Salt and Battery

Curl Up and Dye

First Comes Death Then Comes Marriage

Box Set 1

Box Set 2

Box Set 3

The Gravediggers

The Darkest Corner

Gone to Dust

Say No More